CHERRY AMES NURSE STORIES

CHERRY AMES
SENIOR NURSE

By

HELEN WELLS

SPRINGER PUBLISHING COMPANY

New York

Springer Publishing Company, LLC
11 West 42nd Street, 15th Floor
New York, NY 10036-8002

Production Editor: Print Matters, Inc.
Cover design by Takeout Graphics, Inc.
Composition: Compset, Inc.

Library of Congress Cataloging-in-Publication Data

Wells, Helen
    Cherry Ames, senior nurse / by Helen Wells.
        p. cm. — (Cherry Ames nurse stories)
    Summary: During their final year of training, Cherry Ames and her
friends at Spencer Hospital face difficult decisions about their futures
as nurses during wartime.
    ISBN: 978-0-8261-5604-4 (paperback)
    [1. Nurses—Fiction. 2. Hospitals—Fiction. 3. World War,
1939–1945—Fiction.] I. Title.

PZ7.W4644Cq 2005
[Fic]—dc22

2005051738

Printed in the United States of America.

Contents

~~~~~~

~~~~~~

Foreword

Helen Wells, the author of the Cherry Ames stories, said, "I've always thought of nursing, and perhaps you have, too, as just about the most exciting, important, and rewarding, profession there is. Can you think of any other skill that is *always* needed by everybody, everywhere?"

I was and still am a fan of Cherry Ames. Her courageous dedication to her patients; her exciting escapades; her thirst for knowledge; her intelligent application of her nursing skills; and the respect she achieved as a registered nurse (RN) all made it clear to me that I was going to follow in her footsteps and become a nurse—nothing else would do. Thousands of other young people were motivated by Cherry Ames to become RNs as well. Cherry Ames motivated young people on into the 1970s, when the series ended. Readers who remember reading these books in the past will enjoy rereading them now—whether or not they chose nursing as a career—and perhaps sharing them with others.

My career has been a rich and satisfying one, during which I have delivered babies, saved lives, and cared for people in hospitals and in their homes. I have worked at the bedside and served as an administrator. I have published journals, written articles, taught students, consulted, and given expert testimony. Never once did I regret my decision to enter nursing.

During the time that I was publishing a nursing journal, I became acquainted with Robert Wells, brother of Helen Wells. In the course of conversation I learned that Ms. Wells had passed on and left the Cherry Ames copyright to Mr. Wells. Because there is a shortage of nurses here in the US today, I thought, "Why not bring Cherry back to motivate a whole new generation of young people? Why not ask Mr. Wells for the copyright to Cherry Ames?" Mr. Wells agreed, and the republished series is dedicated both to Helen Wells, the original author, and to her brother Robert Wells who transferred the rights to me. I am proud to ensure the continuation of Cherry Ames into the twenty-first century.

The final dedication is to you, both new and old

readers of Cherry Ames: It is my dream that you enjoy Cherry's nursing skills as well as her escapades. I hope that young readers will feel motivated to choose nursing as your life's work. Remember, as Helen Wells herself said: there's no other skill that's *"always* needed by everybody, everywhere."

Harriet Schulman Forman, RN, Ed.D.
Series Editor

~~~~~~

CHAPTER I

Senior Year

THE RISING BELL CLANGED. CHERRY CAREFULLY wrapped the covers around her ears, turned over and went back to sleep.

When she awoke again, her eyes fell on the clock and she leaped wildly out of bed. She had overslept a whole half-hour! It was *really* late! Half-asleep, she dashed automatically for the maple chest of drawers and collided with a chair instead. Then Cherry remembered. Of course—this wasn't her old room—this was her new room in Crowley, the residence for seniors and graduate nurses! Starting this morning she was a senior—and she was late! Cherry scrambled into her clothes as the clock ticked loudly and warningly. She ran to the closet and pulled out a crisp blue and white striped uniform, with black chevrons on the shoulder.

Late or not, Cherry stopped for breath and a moment's gloating over those senior chevrons.

Then she dashed over to the mirror and slammed her nurse's cap on her head. A breathless girl of twenty looked back at her—a slim, lovely girl with black eyes and black curls, and cheeks and lips so red they had earned her her name. She struggled to get her apron tied, but the bow balked. Outside in the corridor, instead of the usual bedlam of nurses, there was a profound silence—they all had left for breakfast long ago! "It's still me," Cherry marveled at her reflection. "Cherry Ames, from Hilton, Illinois, a senior and not changed a bit! Still tardy!"

She swept up her bandage scissors from where they lay on her radio. That radio was a proud sign of her brand-new estate, for Spencer Nursing School allowed only seniors and graduate nurses to have radios. The clock ticked louder than ever. Cherry raced out of her room, dashed down the stairs and burst out of Crowley's front door. Far away, Cherry made out white figures leaving the dining room, not entering it. "Late, late, always late!" she mourned. "And I'm starving!"

But the nurses' dining room in Spencer Hall, at the far end of the yard, was a good ten minutes' walk away, she figured hungrily. And Cherry's new assignment— her first ward duty as a senior!—was way down at the other end of the yard. Her friend Ann Evans, who was assigned there too, probably already was on the ward. "Q.E.D. no breakfast," Cherry thought, and started off at a sprint.

It was a sunny, bright blue morning, already hot at seven o'clock. Cherry hurried down the flagstone path past the many white hospital buildings, calling good morning to brisk passing nurses and internes. This was her world, she had earned a place in it, and she loved it. That is, it was her world provided she could survive her senior year. Cherry knew that this morning she was embarking on the hardest of all her three years nurses training, and was facing the severest tests so far. She tried to think some serious thoughts about it. But all she could think of was the gnawing in her stomach. She told herself sternly, as she rounded the corner to the Pediatrics Clinic, that the gnawing came from hunger and not from nervousness. She was not scared about a new and very difficult type of ward duty—Children's Ward—certainly not!

Cherry ran up the steps of the Children's Clinic with her full blue and white skirt swirling around her, her crisp white apron crackling, and one hand anchoring her pert white cap. Puffing, she got into the ground floor just in time to see the elevator disappear upwards.

The dispensary with its rows of benches, its desks and filing cabinets, its cubicles of examination rooms, was deserted. Within two hours, it would be overflowing and noisy with clinic patients. Small boys and girls who had managed to get themselves banged up, battered, scratched, out of joint, or were on their way to being sick, would be treated here and sent home, with instructions and medication, and perhaps with orders to come back. Next door in the Babies' Clinic, there would be expectant mothers, wisely being checked up periodically, and eagerly attending the Prenatal class in how to make hygienic preparations at home for the babies who were on their way.

"That's a class I'd like to teach," Cherry thought ambitiously, "either here in a clinic, or as a visiting nurse going right straight into people's homes. That would be fun."

But her new Children's Ward should be fun, she thought, *if* she ever got there. Where was that elevator? She looked anxiously up the shaft.

Finally the car slid down, and Cherry squeezed in. Most of the car was taken up by a large steam wagon full of breakfast for the patients. Cherry's mouth watered. The wagon was in charge of a small stooped woman wearing a maid's black dress and white apron. Her old eyes, in their network of wrinkles, were bright and friendly as a robin's. The elevator operator disappeared for the morning newspapers.

"Top of the morning to you, Miss Ames," the little maid sang out. "Sure, and I know you! Doesn't the whole of Spencer Hospital know the girl who's always so full of fun and——"

"What's *your* name?" Cherry interrupted hastily.

The little maid beamed at her. "I'm Lucy from the Children's Ward. You may have heard of *me*, for Lucy is the children's friend. And it will be a great happiness to have you on my ward." As Cherry's eyes widened, she added, "There's not much going on on her own ward that Lucy does not know!" She lowered her voice mysteriously. "I'll bet you'll never guess what I've got in this-here old wagon for the children. Besides breakfast, I mean to say. Ah, come on now, guess!"

Cherry guessed, for she had heard of the unlikely things Lucy lugged around in that steam wagon, despite hospital regulations. "A geranium? A picture book? A— let's see—some new crayons?"

"I have got one straggly geranium. But look at this!" Lucy raised the lid of an unheated compartment and lifted out a wriggling white rabbit. "Wait till the young ones see that!" The elevator man was returning, so she hastily stuffed the bunny back in the wagon.

As the elevator rose leisurely, Cherry choked with laughter. "It's a lovely idea, Lucy, but what will the head nurse say?" She knew she should say more. She should, especially as a senior nurse, either forbid Lucy to take the rabbit on the ward or warn the head nurse. Cherry could not do it. She knew she was not even going to tell her side-kick Ann Evans about it, for Ann was conscientious enough to shoo Lucy and her rabbit away. "I'm a senior now, I mustn't indulge in monkey business," Cherry thought. But visions of the rabbit leading the doctors and nurses a merry chase convulsed her as she entered the new ward.

At the threshold Cherry caught her breath and stopped to smile. This ward was certainly different from the usual long, plain, white room! She had seen Children's Ward before, but she had forgotten how gay it was. It was a square room, with a great many sunny windows barred at the bottom, and its walls were tinted a cheerful pale yellow, with Mother Goose figures chasing one another merrily around the room. All the furniture was small-scale, including the white iron beds, cribs, and the two tables and the chairs at one end of the ward. The tables were set, now, with tiny pink and blue dishes and silverware and—obviously the pride of the children—tiny milk pitchers which they could pour themselves. Cherry loved it.

She went over to the head nurse's desk to introduce herself and to report on duty. The gray-haired head nurse, Mrs. Crofts, looked up pleasantly. "I'm glad to have you on my ward, Miss Ames," she said. "I hope you will enjoy working with children. They offer some special problems."

"I like children," Cherry said hopefully but uncertainly. "I'd like to learn about nursing them."

"Good," Mrs. Crofts said. "This is Miss George, the nurse on our ward." Cherry found a plump, comfortable, middle-aged woman smiling at her. "And this is the other student nurse, Miss Evans," the head nurse said as Ann came down the row of beds.

Cherry looked affectionately at Ann. She was a calm young woman with brown hair and steady dark blue eyes. Her quiet voice had Cherry's own Middle West twang as she said with a straight face, "How do you do, Miss Ames."

Cherry grinned. "Miss Evans and I have already met."

Miss George showed Cherry and Ann where the ward's serving kitchen, laboratory or utility room, and linen closet were located. Ann's whisper put Cherry's mind back on her work:

"Miss George and Mrs. Crofts and Lucy too— they're all so easy-going and gentle and affectionate and—and reassuring. A child would feel *safe* and loved with them."

Cherry nodded. She wondered if she herself had enough of those qualities and whether she could learn, in time, to handle a whole roomful of sick and emotionally upset children. She was to find out immediately, for the head nurse leading her down the row of small beds told her:

"These six little boys and girls are to be your patients."

Mrs. Crofts described their ailments briefly, at the same time showing Cherry the charts which hung at each child's bedside: a cardiac case, a gastric disorder, rheumatic fever, for this was a Medical Ward. There were no contagious diseases here, no surgical cases convalescing from operations, no broken bones or paralysis cases. Cherry knew that these would be, respectively, on Contagious, Surgical, and Orthopedic Wards. She smiled at the six solemn children who were to be her charges for the coming week. Her smile was a bit anxious.

Ann, on the other side of the ward, was going through the same procedure with Miss George. Cherry met Ann in the kitchen a few minutes later, where they prepared breakfast trays with food from Lucy's wagon. The usual dumbwaiter was missing here. Cherry noted that the rabbit had disappeared from the wagon, but she was too busy with the trays to wonder where it was now. Ann's voice said aloud exactly what Cherry was thinking:

"Our first senior assignment isn't going to be easy."

"Annie, I'm scared," Cherry said. "I wish I already had a graduate's black velvet ribbon on my cap to *prove* I've got all it takes to be a nurse."

Ann slid another tray over to her. "Cheer up, my little worrier. I'm scared too. But we've struggled through this far, maybe we'll wiggle through senior year too."

"It's going to get tougher and tougher," Cherry groaned. "I just know something terrible is going to happen to me."

"Have a cracker," Ann consoled her practically. "At least with your mouth full you can't say such doleful things."

Cherry mumbled with her mouth crammed with cracker, "Nurses are forbidden to eat on the ward, Evans. Anyhow, if I just work hard in our Pediatrics lectures—" she swallowed the cracker and caught the tray Ann slid down "—I'll survive children and babies. Or should I say they'll survive me?"

Ann picked up two trays, small size, and shook her head at Cherry from the kitchen doorway. "Well, if and when anything terrible happens to you, let me know. I always like to be in on the fun."

Cherry hurled a towel at her, missed, picked up her own trays and started out, not too blithely, to the ward.

For a while her small patients were mercifully busy with their breakfasts. There was some spilling of cereal, and one glass of orange juice was overturned, but otherwise they fended for themselves quite well. Then

Cherry took a deep breath and started down her row of beds, to give the small fry their morning baths and to take morning temperature, pulse, and respiration. The night nurse had taken an earlier T.P.R. and had washed faces before breakfast.

"Can I have dinner at the little table?" said six-year-old Jimmy, as he wriggled under the wash cloth which Cherry firmly applied despite his squirming. "Can I, huh?"

"We-ell, hurry up and get well faster," Cherry said, consulting his chart. "Then Dr. Hill will say you can get out of bed."

"I'm hurrying all I can," Jimmy protested. He tugged at her bib. "Ah, please, Miss Ames."

"You aren't hurrying, either. You didn't eat your prunes just now, and you made an awful fuss about swallowing your medicine."

Jimmy dropped his eyes and wrapped one small fist in the sheet. "Okay," he said. "I'll eat 'em." He grinned at her suddenly, and Cherry blew out a big sigh of relief. She had said and done the right things—so far.

At the next bed Cherry had to lean far over the crib bars and struggle with her small and lively patient. Carlotta, aged four, the child of gypsy parents, was not used to conventional clothes and did not approve of them. She had blithely discarded her nightgown and garbed herself in her blanket.

"Cigarette," she welcomed the thermometer and held it in her mouth at a tipsy angle. Then, when Cherry took it away, "No washing. Candy!" she demanded.

"Washing, then a surprise," Cherry dodged. "Hold still, you little scamp!" For Carlotta was entertaining herself by yanking her own black curls, blacker even than Cherry's. "And on goes the nightgown—" Carlotta opened her mouth wide to protest. Cherry dived into her apron pocket and hastily held out two bright-colored hair bows, stowed there for emergency. "Choose!"

Carlotta chose the red one, and Cherry tied it in her hair. That over, Carlotta again opened her mouth. One howl might set the whole ward to howling. Cherry said desperately, "Want to play with this?" and thrust the green hair bow, too, into the small hands. Carlotta settled down, a small rakish figure of pride and satisfaction.

Mary Ruth, in the next bed, obediently submitted to Cherry's quick ministrations without a word. "She's too quiet," Cherry thought, placing her fingers on the tiny wrist, and watching the little girl's breathing. That's not obedience, that's listlessness." She wrote down the heightened temperature and pulse on the chart, and signaled the head nurse with her eyes.

"I feel bad," Mary Ruth whispered in a frightened voice. "I want my mother, Miss Ames." She nestled her hot head against Cherry's shoulder. Cherry quickly put her arm about the child, realizing that children need affection as much as they need food and care to get well.

"I'll try to have your mother come, Mary Ruth, but I can't promise." She knew she must be scrupulously honest with children, to keep their trust. "In the meantime, there's a teddy bear over in the toy closet who looks lonesome. He spoke to me this morning about finding him a playmate."

Mary Ruth's round eyes slowly changed expression. "Ho, he didn't say that! A teddy bear can't talk! But can I play with him?"

"I'll send him over the moment I finish taking his temperature," Cherry agreed. Mary Ruth lay back on the pillow contentedly.

Three more small patients—five-year-old Thomas, who insisted that Cherry call him Thomas, not Tom; six-year-old Burton, who would be into mischief the moment he was convalescing, Cherry suspected; and Amy, calm-mannered and roly-poly, who at seven already had a matronly air. Cherry got her small regiment bathed and checked up without mishap.

Cherry stopped for breath and gingerly congratulated herself. She was looking about to see how Ann had fared, when the head nurse called her over.

"Yes, Mrs. Crofts?"

Her day's orders came now. But first the head nurse said, "That was very nicely done, Miss Ames. You're a competent nurse and you seem to have a special knack with children."

"Thank you, Mrs. Crofts," Cherry said quietly. But inside she glowed with pleasure.

"Now, then. You're getting another little boy this morning. We'll put him on isolation for several days. Then if it is all right, we'll bring him in with the other children, so he won't be too lonesome."

Cherry nodded and hurried to air and dust one of the small private rooms, and make up the miniature bed with fresh linens.

She had a difficult half-hour when the new little boy was admitted. He was frightened of the new surroundings, terrified of being sick, and heartbroken when he saw his mother leave. He wept. Cherry finally soothed him with a battered old tin train brought from home, which he apparently cherished. She made him completely happy by *not* insisting that he eat the special diet she brought in—with the result that, when she returned half an hour later, he had eaten every mouthful.

"Senior, you got over that hurdle too," Cherry marveled to herself. She stole one more moment to notice that neither Lucy nor the rabbit was in sight. She suspected that Lucy was shifting the rabbit around a good deal.

Then Cherry rushed—rushed through the dozens of chores there are to do on a ward: treatments, reports, and errands, then noon dinner for her patients and a mad dash for her own dinner, then afternoon care and back rubbing. The day flew along. Suddenly to her surprise it was mid-afternoon, time for the resident doctor's visit. And here was Dr. Hill, a pleasant-looking man, walking into the ward.

But it was the young doctor bursting in with Dr. Hill who seized Cherry's attention. He came hurtling around the corner and all but knocked her down.

"Why don't you watch where you're going?" he demanded as he collected the soiled towels she had been carrying.

Cherry's eyes and cheeks blazed. "Watch out yourself!"

"Pretty quick-tempered, aren't you?" He had a striking face, beak-nosed and jaggedly hewn, full of character and humor. His eyes, under decided black brows, were golden brown. His hair was much lighter, almost sandy color, and unmanageably straight. His jaw was uncompromisingly square.

Cherry counted to ten under her breath lest Mrs. Crofts and Dr. Hill, examining charts at the desk, overhear her. Then she looked straight back at him. He was not a great deal taller than she was, but he was as solid and strong as an oak tree. "I think you have the quick temper in question," she said and righted her nurse's cap.

"I'm sorry," the young man said, not sounding overly contrite. "At least I can carry your towels to the laundry chute for you."

Before she could say anything, he took them out of her hands. He strode off as if he had conquered the earth and now owned it, leaving Cherry to hurry after him down the aisle of beds. That bold male walk of his infuriated Cherry. He had the darnedest air of being someone special, she thought.

Cherry opened her mouth to demand her towels back. But he dumped them down the chute, grinned at her, and disappeared after Dr. Hill and the head nurse into the new little boy's room. The door closed.

Cherry promptly returned to the ward and busied herself remaking an empty bed. It was too bad Ann had gone to the apothecary to get a prescription filled—Cherry needed to explode to somebody. A few minutes later the young visiting doctor came surging in.

Nurse!" he called. "Dr. Hill would like a dressing cart!"

Cherry thought in exasperation. "Just as if he had never seen me before." Aloud she said, as cool and impersonal as he, "I'll get it immediately, Doctor."

"He's in a hurry, Nurse!"

Cherry whirled. "I said *immediately*, Doctor!" She marched off. There were no dressings to change on Medical Ward; she would have to borrow a dressing cart from the general supply closet which Surgical also used. Cherry wondered why Dr. Hill wanted it. The new little boy was on Medical to be built up for an operation. But Dr. Hill must have found on the child a cut or scratch which needed sterile cleansing and medication and bandaging.

"Can't you hurry, Nurse?" The young doctor was right behind her. Cherry bit her tongue to keep from replying. She sharply turned the corner; he came right on her heels. He looked at the wheeled cart, with its solutions, gauze, sterile forceps, and big basins for soiled dressings, and sniffed. "It doesn't look very well kept!"

"It's in apple-pie order and you know it!" Cherry burst out indignantly.

He leaned against the wall and a smile spread over his forceful intelligent face. "That's better," he grinned at her. "At least you're paying some attention to me. It seems I have to get you furious to make you even look at me."

Cherry could not help smiling. He was maddening, this extraordinary, thoroughly masculine, young doctor, and she liked him.

"Could I interest you in having tea with me?" he said.

Cherry suppressed a smile. "You certainly are in a hurry to get acquainted, Doctor."

He glanced at her out of one bright intelligent eye. "You look very nice and I should like to know you and why not come straight to the point?"

She tried to look demure. "The rules, you know, say doctors and nurses attached to the same hospital may meet only professionally."

"Page seven of the handbook," he agreed, undaunted. "But most rules were made to be broken. I've found a restaurant near here where they have all the fancy cakes girls like——"

"—and you've taken at least a dozen nurses to tea there already," Cherry interrupted mischievously.

He turned around and looked her emphatically full in the eyes. "No, I have not," he said, "and will not." For the first time, she saw what a serious person he was, under his boldness and bantering. She saw, too, a flicker of sensitivity as he added, "I don't mean to press you into an acquaintance with an utter stranger."

"There, there," Cherry said, laughing. "If we're going to work together in the same hospital, we won't be strangers for long." She gave the dressing cart a little push. "Didn't you say Dr. Hill was in a hurry?" she teased.

"I was right," he said cheerfully. "You *are* nice. Don't bother wheeling in the cart. Dr. Hill doesn't really need it."

Cherry laughed at him. To cover his embarrassment, he idly uncovered and re-covered a few things on the cart.

Suddenly, out of nowhere—but actually, out of the largest covered basin—flew a white streak. It leaped in the air and scuttled madly around the supply closet. The young doctor dashed after it, but it eluded his outstretched hand.

"What's that thing?" he demanded as he sprinted around the closet, chasing the white streak.

"It's a—a rabbit," Cherry said faintly.

"A what? I thought you said that cart was in apple-pie order!"

Cherry abruptly sank down on a stool and whooped with laughter.

"Look!" she gasped, holding her aching sides. "There it goes!" She pointed, helpless with mirth, to the open door. Like a white shadow, the rabbit was flying down the corridor, headed for the ward. The young doctor raced after it, his white coat flapping.

By the time Cherry could stop laughing a little and return to the ward she found it in an uproar. The frightened rabbit raced up and down under the rows of beds. Dr. Hill swooped at it from one end of the room, trying to seize it as it flashed by. The head nurse and the graduate nurse were running along with it as best they could. Ann and Lucy were down on their hands and knees. The young doctor ran beside the rabbit, or now behind it, wildly flapping a towel. The delighted children were shrieking at the tops of their voices.

Finally the rabbit made a sharp right turn, leaped clear across Carlotta's crib, and fled down the hall out of sight.

Gradually the laughter petered out to a few suppressed chokings and giggles, and then to a tentative silence. Out of Cherry's guilty enjoyment, the grayhaired head nurse spoke.

"Where did that rabbit come from?"

Mrs. Crofts glanced knowingly at Lucy the maid, and so did Cherry. The little old woman looked terrified. Cherry took her senior life in her hands and said courageously:

"I found it in the dressing cart," No one said anything. Cherry added helpfully, "Stuffed in a pot."

Everyone suddenly howled again, including the head nurse. Ann was bent double. Even Lucy managed a woebegone smile. Cherry raised her voice to be heard over the laughter. "It was my fault, Mrs. Crofts. I saw it first. If I'd shut the door, it would not have got away."

"Never mind," Dr. Hill said as he turned to leave. "That rabbit has broken hospital routine, but it's done the children a lot of good."

"Someone," said the head nurse, still breathless, "had better let the poor little creature out of the building."

"I'll do it," the young doctor offered and, after a quick smile at Cherry, he was gone.

Cherry realized then that she did not even know his name. And since he was only a visitor today, he would not be returning to the ward. Well, it was time for her and Ann to go off the ward themselves. She saw Lucy's grateful smile and nodded. Then she and Ann reported off duty to the head nurse. Cherry thanked her for being lenient about the rabbit.

Mrs. Crofts smiled, but she said, "A senior really must be a little more sober and responsible."

When she got out into the elevator with Ann, Cherry said, "Oh, shucks, who wants to be a senior anyway?"

CHAPTER II

Dreams and Plans

BECOMING A SENIOR TOOK UP THE REST OF CHERRY'S afternoon. She moved the balance of her belongings from her old room, in the residence hall for first-year and junior student nurses, to the grandeur of Crowley. Her little room looked very attractive when she had put everything neatly away. Cherry set photographs of her parents and of her twin brother Charlie, and a snapshot of young Midge Fortune, on the table beside the chintz-covered daybed. She wanted to write to them all and tell them she was safely a senior—maybe she could squeeze that in this evening, after studying.

Cherry looked at their pictures rather wistfully. She missed them. She missed her own neighborly tree-shaded little town of Hilton, and the rich corn and wheat countryside where she had grown up. She especially missed Charlie, who had given her the nurse's watch which she so proudly wore on her wrist. She wondered about Charlie; his letter this morning announced matter-of-factly that he might not be returning to the State University this September. Instead, he was hoping to be accepted in the Army Air Force. He wanted, he wrote, to train either as a pilot or for the more urgent job of aerial gunner.

"You always did have your heart set on being a flier," Cherry said to the young man in the picture. Her twin brother was a very masculine and startlingly blond version of Cherry herself. "And you always were determined to live up to your plans. Well, heaven knows, we need fliers to win this war—and nurses too."

She turned to the photographs of her parents: her father a businesslike, good-humored looking man; her mother, sweet-faced and still young. Then she studied the new snapshot of Midge, Dr. Fortune's motherless daughter. Midge was fifteen now, growing tall and graceful. "But you're still the same wild Indian," Cherry grinned. It comforted her, somehow, to see their familiar faces and have this imaginary visit with them, in the midst of the excitement and strain of taking on senior status.

She put their pictures back in place now. She brushed her black curls until they shone, tried to tone down her crimson cheeks with powder, and slipped on a crisp fresh apron for supper. Fresh and glowing as a red rose, she started to walk across the yard to Spencer Hall.

Cherry loved the yard at this twilight hour. That brief surge of homesickness disappeared, for the hospital was her real home. White-clad nurses and internes called greetings to her as they hurried down the paths from one building to another. In the many windows, lights would soon be going on. Something between happiness and sorrow welled up in Cherry. It was something very sweet, almost too poignant to bear. She loved this hospital so! She loved its quiet white wards full of patients, its tiny kitchens, the busy utility rooms, the cool gray laboratory, the hushed white corridors smelling of soapsuds, the ambulances clanging up before Emergency Ward, this green wandering yard dotted with buildings which housed special branches of medicine.

Most of all, Cherry loved nursing itself. Her dream was the dream of being a nurse, of helping people on a grand scale in the most important way there is. She had come to believe in it through Dr. Joe's practical idealism, and she always would believe in it.

At the entrance to Spencer Hall, the great stately central building of Spencer Hospital, someone seized her arm.

"I hear you're having Welsh rabbit for supper!" Gwen Jones stood there laughing—a sturdy girl with bright red hair, a few freckles, and a merry Puck's face.

"So Ann told you all!" Cherry laughed back.

"As a doctor's daughter, let me say that your behavior was most undignified, Miss Ames." Gwen tried to glare but she was not very successful. She shoved back her short red hair and added candidly, "May I also say that from my years of assisting the medico of a coal mining town, to wit, my Dad, I'll be human first and dignified second."

"Bravo!" Cherry said. "Do we stand around making speeches or do we get some nourishment?" They went into the nurses' dining room.

It was a large attractive room, decorated in peach and green, cafeteria arrangement. There were tables for four and for eight, and one long table lined with brand-new and painfully self-conscious probationers. The room was crowded with young women in probationer's gray, bibless and capless; in student blue and white set off with rustling white aprons, crisp white caps, and demure black shoes and stockings; and in the head-to-toe white of the graduate nurse. The whole room pulsed with talk and laughter and the vitality of these purposeful young women.

Cherry and Gwen got their trays appetizingly laden, then went in search of Ann. They found her at a round table with big Bertha Larsen, little ivory-faced Mai Lee, Josie Franklin, Marie Swift, and the girl who had once been Cherry's enemy, Vivian Warren. As Cherry sat down, she felt grateful that these girls whom she had known since her probie days were not among those classmates dropped at the beginning of senior year.

"Look, kids," Vivian Warren laughed. "As mighty seniors, they could dine in glory with graduates! But they're sitting with us. You must love us."

"We do," Cherry said briskly. "Did you get your Spencer scholarship again this year, Vivi?" It was no secret that Vivian's family could not afford to send her through nursing school, and Vivian Warren was admired for her spunk and good work which took her through on her own.

Vivian's face, which had once been so hard and suspicious, lighted. "Not only did *I* get it! But do you girls know that most of these new students are going to be nurses by courtesy of the U.S. Cadet Nurse Corps? I wish I were on that kind of scholarship. I'll bet you don't know what all the Cadet Nurses get! They get all their training, and their rooms and meals, and a stunning gray street uniform, all free—not to mention monthly pocket money besides! All you have to do to get it is to apply and qualify! Pretty wonderful for these girls, I'd say!"

"Pretty wonderful for the taxpayers who provide the scholarships and who'll eventually get a sufficient number of A-1 nurses in return," Marie Swift said matter-of-factly. Marie was a wealthy girl who found nursing the most thrilling thing she had ever tried. "It's a big job to keep a country healthy. Not to mention keeping the armed services whole and well. And after the war, nurses will be needed more than ever. Nursing isn't just a temporary wartime job. A nurse has a future."

Bertha Larsen leaned forward, her round face troubled. "Ah, those poor little probies! They're so lost here, just like we were. It breaks my heart! I wish I could help them or something."

Josie Franklin gave a slight shriek. The others turned in alarm. Josie peered at them timidly from behind her glasses. "Cherry! Don't you remember what you said? At the end of our first year? We were in the dining room—I think we had shrimp salad that night—it was just before we walked over to the lake where the seniors throw their black stockings when they——"

Cherry exchanged a grin with quiet demure Mai Lee. "One thing at a time, please. What did I say about shrimp salad and black stockings that has anything to do with the sufferings of probationers?"

"Well, it wasn't about shrimp salad exactly, but you said we ought to—well, when we became seniors—sort of each one of us adopt a probationer. We're seniors now. I mean one apiece, that is." Josie's thin face was very earnest.

Suddenly the girls all were talking at once. "That's right, Cherry did think that up!" "We'd suffered so ourselves that—" "And it's not such a bad idea either!"

They all turned on Cherry point-blank and demanded, "Shall we adopt them, Cherry?"

Cherry's stomach rapidly sank. She tried to retire behind a large piece of bread and butter. But her classmates were demanding an answer. She said weakly, "Suppose they don't want to be adopted in the first place? Suppose my probationer thinks I'm the worst nurse in the senior class? Those government Cadet Nurse Corps scholarships are for girls seventeen to thirty-five—how'd you like to adopt someone thirty-five? Suppose——"

"Never mind supposing!" Ann interrupted. "You thought this up in the beginning, Cherry Ames. Speak up!"

"And make it good!" Gwen warned.

Cherry stared at her plate, thinking, then said slowly, "You know, in a year we're going to be graduated and most of us will leave Spencer for good. I guess our class would like to leave something behind us—some gift to the school or some tradition. Most all the other classes do. And this year is the last chance for us." She studied their listening faces, one by one. "So if you want to, and if the rest of our class wants to——"

"They'll want to!" Bertha Larsen cried. "I'll ask them right now!"

She and Ann and Vivian and Marie promptly got up and circulated around the dining room. A loud buzz of talk arose. Cherry waited. Five minutes later they returned.

"They want to!" Bertha announced. "The seniors are dying to adopt the probies!"

Mai Lee rapped gently on the table for order. "I propose that Cherry apply to the Superintendent of Nurses for permission."

Cherry groaned. The others all assured her hastily that they would be standing outside Miss Reamer's office, lending moral support, if she felt too weak.

"All right," said Cherry, scrambling to her feet. "But don't say I didn't warn you!"

She turned the corner out of the nurses' dining room, went through Spencer's vast rotunda, and turned another corner to the Superintendent's office. She raised her hand to knock on Miss Reamer's door and paused. She felt worried, astonished, topsy-turvy, and hilarious.

"I still don't know what being a senior is," she thought, "but I never expected it to include rabbits and a pint-size gypsy and that extraordinary young doctor and—and now, adopting people!"

~~~~~~

CHAPTER III

Two Strange People

A WEEK LATER AN ANNOUNCEMENT APPEARED ON THE nurses' bulletin board. The Superintendent of Nurses herewith granted permission to the seniors to "adopt" the entering class of probationers. Miss Reamer invited all seniors and probationers to a tea in Spencer lounge that afternoon between three and four.

"The old darling, giving us a tea party," Cherry said to Ann. They tucked in their small patients in the Children's Ward and rushed back to Crowley to change.

Cherry arrived at Miss Reamer's tea, breathless and flushed, in a saucily starched uniform. The big lounge in Spencer was overflowing with seniors, trying to look kind and reassuring, and beside them were young probationers in their gray dresses, painfully shy. Cherry made her way through the stiff little groups with their tea cups, stealing glances at Gwen and Ann and Vivian and Marie Swift, each with her probie in tow. It was hard to tell anything from their polite faces. Only Ann seemed really at ease and warmly friendly. Well, most things were difficult at the beginning, Cherry thought.

She went up to the long flower-strewn tea table, where at one end Miss Reamer sat behind a decorative samovar, dispensing tea and cakes. At the other end of the table, the flinty-faced Assistant Superintendent of Nurses, Miss Kent, poured, looking as if she would be a good deal happier in an Operating Room.

"Good afternoon, Miss Reamer," Cherry said, with genuine pleasure at seeing the older woman. "Have you a probationer for me?" In order to be perfectly impartial, Miss Reamer had acted as agent between the two classes, picking names of seniors and probies out of a hat. Cherry was anxious to know whom she herself had drawn.

"Hello, Miss Ames. Yes, your probationer's name is Mildred Burnham. She isn't here yet." Cherry accepted the cup which Miss Reamer held out to her. "I don't understand why not. All the probationers were dismissed in plenty of time for the tea."

Cherry felt a quick misgiving. Cherry was, conspicuously, the only unattached senior in the room. She waited around, pretending to serve cake, and finally went to sit down with Vivian and Gwen. Two girls in gray were with them. They were so frozen with respect for seniors that they could not say much beyond "Yes" and "No" and "Thank you." But they were clearly eager for the sympathetic help which Vivian and Gwen offered.

"They're sweet," Cherry thought as Gwen introduced the probationers. "I hope mine measures up to these two."

"We were just talking about Marius Lexington Upham," Gwen informed her.

"What?" said Cherry incredulously. "What's that, a race horse or a battleship?" The smaller of the two probies giggled.

Vivian said, "Believe it or not, that's the poor chap's name." Cherry only half listened, watching the door in some embarrassment.

"Poor chap, indeed!" Gwen sputtered. She shook her red head admiringly. "He's got this hospital on its ear! The worst of it is, nobody can handle him! Even the senior staff men admit he's absolutely brilliant—and absolutely headstrong! He's untameable!"

"Gwen dear, you'll frighten the probies," Cherry said idly. "No one can be——"

"Oh, can't he?" Vivian cut in. "Did you ever meet a cyclone? Of all the extraordinary——"

Just then Miss Reamer called Cherry over. Her attention swerved to the unknown probationer who was to be her personal charge for the coming year. She rose and excused herself.

Standing beside the Superintendent of Nurses at the table was a girl of about eighteen with a dumpy figure and an ordinary face. She would have made no impression whatsoever on Cherry, except for the unpleasant way she seemed to draw herself away from everyone around her.

Cherry took an instant dislike to her.

Then she realized it and was appalled. "I've no right to a prejudice! I don't even know the girl," Cherry scolded herself as Miss Reamer introduced them.

"How do you do," said Mildred Burnham. Her face was heavy with indifference and hostility. The girl was like a dead weight.

"I'll have to win her over," Cherry thought, feeling weary right at the start. What was bothering this girl? Cherry swallowed her dislike and made an effort.

"Wouldn't you like to sit down? I can't guarantee finding an empty sofa, but I do see a couple of chairs."

"It makes no difference to me," Mildred Burnham said flatly.

"Well, it makes a difference to me," Cherry said and managed a laugh. "I've been on my feet since seven this morning, and you know they say a nurse never stands when she can sit, and never sits when she can lie down."

"Do they say that?" Mildred Burnham said. She followed Cherry to the vacant chairs and they sat down.

Cherry groped for something that this leaden girl might respond to. "What sort of class are you in?" she asked.

"They're nothing wonderful," Mildred Burnham said.

Cherry gulped and tried again to see something about her probie that she could like.

"You're a poised probationer. It's exceptional. But honestly, aren't you excited inside about starting training?"

The girl looked at her out of stony eyes. "Excited? No. I mean to be a nurse, but I don't see why I should get wild-eyed about it."

Cherry hung on tight to her temper and stared in bewilderment at her adoptee. Mildred Burnham suddenly sat up straight in her chair.

"You needn't think you can patronize me," she cried, "just because you're two years ahead of me!"

So that was it. How childish! How absurd! Cherry said quickly:

"Honestly I don't feel the least bit patronizing. I certainly would have no reason to. I want you to accept whatever help I can give, in the way I mean it."

But Mildred Burnham's sullen expression did not waver. She preserved a hateful silence. Cherry's patience began to give out.

"Perhaps you'd rather some other senior adopted you?"

"It makes no difference."

"Or would you rather not be adopted at all?"

"Oh, no. I expect that this adoption business will be useful to me. Do you mind if I go now?"

Cherry's patience reached its end. "You're very rude," she said sharply. "If you're going to be a nurse, you'll have to learn to be civil. You might as well start with me."

"Thanks so much for the advice," said Mildred Burnham sarcastically.

Cherry wondered what her blood pressure was at that point. She got to her feet and walked away.

In a moment she felt a little ashamed of herself. She was the older, she at least should keep her temper in hand. She should, for instance, get another cup of tea and return to that insolent girl, instead of letting their first encounter end on a sour note. Get off to a bad start and the year ahead could be unbearable.

But Cherry's feet were taking her to the door and out of the lounge. She could not help it—she really did dislike that girl. In a ruffled temper, she headed for the basement.

Down in the basement, in its dim lights and brick walls, with its blocks-long labyrinth of winding corridors which criss-crossed unexpectedly, Cherry automatically started down the underground short-cut to Crowley. Still under Spencer, she passed the sputum room where tubercular waste articles were carefully burned. She passed busy utility rooms, and the big kitchens. But soon the tunnel she traveled grew deserted. She kept glancing up at the pipes overhead, following the green one. Green pipes carried water, red carried steam, yellow carried gas, and there were two more pipes she could not identify. She passed the last room, the boiler room, and now the tunnel grew narrow. She must be somewhere under the yard. Her footsteps rang out in the stillness.

Suddenly about thirty yards ahead of her a man darted out of the wall. Cherry jumped, then realized he had come from some corridor which she did not know existed. He whirled around wildly, looking hastily in all directions, then came running toward her. Cherry could not make out his face at this distance. He wore no white coat but a dark business suit, and he was powerfully built. The thought crossed her mind that he might be an escaped patient from Psychiatric. Or he might be an hysterical patient trying to run away. She ordered herself not to be frightened: a nurse knew many ways to handle hysterical people. Nevertheless Cherry glanced behind her: the tunnel back to Spencer stretched a silent endless way. The man was running nearer and nearer. He was shouting something at her now and waving his arms. Panic-stricken, Cherry broke into a run, back toward Spencer.

But she could not run fast enough. The man was gaining on her. She could hear his approaching footsteps, heavier than her own, above the crackle of her apron and her own panting. The man cried out again. Suddenly his footsteps rang out faster and harder, and a hand closed on her arm.

Cherry, dripping with perspiration, swayed against the wall. All she could think was how cold the brick felt against her overheated body. Then her blurred vision cleared and she looked up.

"You idiot," the man was saying. Cherry looked again and blinked. It was the young doctor who had scattered her towels all over the ward and chased Lucy's rabbit! "I merely asked you which way! I was lost."

"Sorry." Cherry's panting was dying down and she relaxed. Then she giggled. "You look wild enough to scare anyone." His sandy-colored hair stood on end, and his emphatic black brows were drawn together.

"Don't tell me—" he started belligerently.

"I'll tell you if I want to!" Cherry shot back. "I don't know what it is about you, but you make me see red!"

He leaned against the wall and grinned happily at her. "It seems that's the way to make you notice me. I'll remember to infuriate you, if necessary." He took out his handkerchief and fanned her with it. "Still scared? Still mad?"

"Well, to be honest, no." They smiled slowly at each other.

"I've been looking high and low for you all week," he announced. "I almost decided you had been a beautiful mirage and didn't actually exist." His keen eyes searched her face. He asked her abruptly, "You aren't afraid of me, are you?"

"Afraid! I'm not even impressed. Why would I be afraid of you?" She drew up her slim figure.

"Never mind. I knew you wouldn't be afraid. I was right about you—right the first minute I saw you."

"This is very interesting," Cherry said out of her astonishment, "but I've got to get along to——"

He waved that aside with a toss of his head. "I want you to promise me something. No, you be quiet a minute—though I must say I like a girl who's got a mind of her own." A smile lightened his serious face, and flickered out. "You're going to hear a lot of stories about me. It's true I'm a strange bird. But I'm not strange the way gossip has it. Don't believe them."

Cherry looked at him with puzzled eyes. "What— what's your name?"

"Lex. Marius Lexington Upham."

Of course! Gwen had been talking about the exceptional new interne—untameable—brilliant cyclone—

Cherry wished she could remember what she had said. She shook her black curls and sighed. "I've adopted one strange bird today already. That's enough."

"Adopt me, too." He was not teasing or joking. His forceful face was dead serious. "It's difficult being a person who doesn't quite fit in. It's lonely."

"I see," Cherry said softly. She thought, "You don't fit in because you're so far above average. I'm sure you *are* lonely." She smiled at him a little. "But why me?" she asked.

"Why not?"

"I haven't much time," she started hesitantly.

"What's time for, if you don't use it to do the things you want?" He shrugged his big shoulders. "If you won't break the rules and have tea with me, will you come and talk with me in the library? We could discuss the cardio-vascular system, you know. Why I could talk with you about the alphabet and find it fascinating."

"But I don't have time even for that. For instance, I promised to help Dr. Fortune occasionally in his laboratory and——"

"Dr. Joseph Fortune? So that's where you spend your free time? In that case," the young man said thoughtfully, "I ought to get myself made his assistant." He looked quite capable of doing it. "Well? Well?" he demanded, his black brows drawing together. "Will you adopt me?"

Cherry burst out laughing. He *was* something like a cyclone. "All right, Lex, consider yourself adopted."

He jammed his hands in his pockets and leaned against the wall and looked extremely pleased.

"And now," he said, "I'll walk you to wherever you're going, so you won't get scared again, you sissy." He gripped her arm firmly and plunged ahead at a rapid pace.

"Wait!" Cherry gasped. "I don't like being dragged along!"

"Keep up with me then," he said. But he slowed his pace down to a more gentle one.

They walked along in comfortable silence. A few yards more, and they had reached the wide basement of Crowley. They paused. Lex asked Cherry when he was going to see her again. She looked at him ruefully.

"Heaven only knows. Every minute of my time is cram-jam full. And you must be working plenty hard yourself."

She was sorry, for she liked this amazing young doctor. She told him so with a warm and tantalizing smile. From the way he looked back at her, he very much approved of her scarlet cheeks and black diamond eyes.

"Never mind. I'll find you," he assured her. "You'll discover you've adopted me in earnest."

Cherry realized with a start that he was serious about being adopted. Adopting Marius Lexington Upham might be like adopting a bomb! She turned and fled upstairs.

In her own quiet little room, Cherry went to the mirror which hung over the chest of drawers. She studied the face that looked back at her.

"It certainly is a comfort," she thought, her head spinning, "after those two crazy people I've adopted, to see someone *normal* again!"

~~~~~~

CHAPTER IV

Very Small Fry

CHERRY'S WORRIES ABOUT LEX AND MILDRED BURNHAM came to a quick and unexpected solution. She simply did not have time to see them. And she lost interest in anyone aged more than two weeks.

There had been a couple of chance breathless meetings with Lex in the yard. Cherry wanted to see Lex; she was curious to know whether his sudden interest in her was a mere temporary impulse. As for Mildred, Cherry promised herself, "I'll *make* time—I'll squeeze her in somehow." But so far she had not succeeded. September already had slipped out of her grasp, tart golden October had arrived, and here was Cherry transferred from Pediatrics upstairs to Obstetrics.

If only Obstetrics had been the usual ward's wild scramble, Cherry would have been too rushed to think of Lex or her probie at all. But Obstetrics was mostly waiting, generally peaceful to the point of being tedious. Cherry grew a little restless. She was going to be on Obstetrics for the student nurse's usual three months' period. The first two weeks, when she had ward duty taking care of the new mothers, was the slowest and least exciting part.

Cherry kept the mothers warm and quiet and comfortable, and coaxed them to eat the things they should. She shooed away proud fathers, excited grand-parents and talkative friends who came too often and stayed too long, exhausting the patients. Cherry rather enjoyed the intimate atmosphere of this ward: it had only ten beds, and the mothers—and the nurses too—formed a sort of sorority in their special interest in babies. There was a bright break in the slow routine when the infants were brought down from the nursery to the ward for feedings, six times a day.

They were packed in a wheeled truck, all ten of them lying in a row. Long before the truck arrived, when the babies' combined squallings, gruntings, bubblings and puffings were just a faint sound down the corridor, a thrill went through the ward. The patients, who had been until now matter-of-fact women, reading or chatting or dozing, suddenly sat up and appeared radiant. The nurses, too, looked eager and amused. Cherry forgot everything else and thoroughly enjoyed herself.

When the two nursery nurses wheeled in the truck, with its tiny lively occupants, the ward came thoroughly to life. Only the babies themselves, the reason for this excitement and happiness, remained nonchalant.

"They get cuter and funnier each time," Cherry said to Miss O'Malley, her fellow nurse, as they each dug squirming tiny babies out of their compartments.

"This one is a little damp," Miss O'Malley said hastily.

Cherry laughed. She did not mind. She had taken to this branch of nursing as easily and blithely and efficiently as if she were a veteran, instead of a student nurse.

Cherry slipped her hand under Baby Norris's warm downy head, rested his spine along her arm, and lifted him up firmly and horizontally, between her hip and arm. He made a compact bundle. He blinked gravely at her, opened his tiny pink mouth in a yawn, then stared up at her again. Each day Cherry made fresh discoveries about these miniature human beings. "Baby Norris is decidedly dignified," she observed.

"Even his mother is awed by him," Miss O'Malley answered. She efficiently scooped up a baby and, with a wriggling blanket on her arm, started toward its mother.

Cherry found one small baby quite an armful, particularly with Baby Norris waving his miniature pink plump fist in her face. Around his wrist, sealed on, was a bead bracelet which spelled out his last name. Even so, as Cherry approached the bed, she glanced at the name on the bed and said aloud, "Baby Norris."

"Are you sure it's my baby?" said the nervous little woman in the bed. "Are you sure you aren't making a mistake?"

"Absolutely sure," Cherry soothed her. "See how fine he looks today." She laid the baby in the curve of his mother's arm, thinking that sometimes a nurse has to be chiefly a psychologist.

"Why does he kick so?" Mrs. Norris asked, touching him gingerly. "Oh, dear, I'll never be able to take care of him at home. I don't know the first thing about babies!" she wailed.

"You'll learn," said Mrs. Sorley from the next bed. She was a big, good-natured, middle-aged woman. "By the time you have your fifth, like me, a baby's no trouble at all." She patted her chunky infant comfortably on the seat of his diaper.

Cherry suppressed her smile at Mrs. Norris's terrified expression and went back to the cart. She took Baby Saunders on her arm and held her a moment. "Hello, my lovely," Cherry murmured. The baby girl's gray eyes were like a china doll's, fringed with black lashes, a golden halo covered her little head, her skin was pink and delicate as a flower. She rested, quiet and good, on Cherry's arm, breathing lightly. "I wish she were mine," Cherry thought as she trotted over to the mother's bed.

Mrs. Saunders reached out her arms. She was only eighteen. Her young husband was fighting somewhere in Europe. Cherry knew that Mrs. Saunders had not heard from him or about him for three months. Yet she had never heard the young mother say anything about her own worry, except what she said now:

"Dick's going to be pretty proud when he sees his daughter."

"I should think so!" Cherry said a hasty little prayer that he might come home safely, that he might some day really see his beautiful little daughter.

The cart was empty now except for Baby Lane. Cherry scooped him up and could not help laughing. He was wrinkled, red, and wiry, more like an animated dried prune, Cherry thought, than a human being. Baby Lane tossed his arms and legs, looked her square in the eye, and grunted for nourishment.

"He's so homely," Mrs. Lane mourned half-humorously as Cherry handed him over and helped her to a more comfortable position in the bed. "My husband is disappointed in such an ugly duckling."

"He's a fine husky boy, and just what most brand-new babies look like," Cherry retorted. "Just wait until his skin grows a little less sensitive and less red, and he gains some fat to go over those muscles."

"I hope he grows better-looking," Mrs. Lane sighed. But from the way she stroked the fuzzy crimson little head, Cherry saw that her remarks had comforted and satisfied her patient.

Cherry and Miss O'Malley patrolled the quiet ward, to see that the mothers did not nurse the babies too fast and to watch for any emergency. Cherry taught one amazed baby to bubble. Then she carried the babies, carefully horizontal, back to the truck. Most of them, now that they were full, were drowsing, tiny hands uncurled, limp and soft and warm. They were packed back into their beds, the truck was wheeled out and the ward settled down to matter-of-fact knitting again until the babies' next visit.

Cherry was still chuckling over the distinct personalities of these tiny people when she went off duty. But the moment she was out of the ward and hurrying across the yard with her nurse's cape billowing out behind her, time pressed at her heels again. Senior lecture classes were heavy, she had an enormous amount of reading to do, and besides she had promised Dr. Joe to help him. She half-ran through the blowing October afternoon toward Lincoln Hall where his laboratory was. Lincoln housed laboratories, a special library, and valuable medical records. Cherry, like all student nurses, and even most young staff doctors and graduate nurses, would have had no business in Lincoln, except that she was helping her old friend and mentor, Dr. Joseph Fortune.

Dr. Fortune had brought the Ames twins into the world, and had been their friend and neighbor all their lives. His selfless devotion to medical research in his little home laboratory in Hilton—in the teeth of poverty and loneliness and lack of recognition, in those days— had inspired Cherry to be a nurse. Cherry had tried to pay him back in her own way. After Mrs. Fortune had died, while Cherry was still in high school, Cherry had kept an eye on impractical Dr. Joe and on his house and on his madcap daughter, Midge. Dr. Joe's present recognition, and his presence here at Spencer, was due to Cherry—and a nightmarish episode in her first year at the nursing school.

Cherry blew into Dr. Joe's small cluttered laboratory, red-cheeked and out of breath. "Why aren't there more hours in the day, Dr. Joe?" she asked in greeting.

Dr. Joe lifted his head from the microscope a full minute after her remark. He brushed the boyish shock of gray hair out of his eye. "What's on your mind, Cherry?" When she shook her head, he said gently, "Oh, yes, there is. I'm not as absent-minded as you think I am. I noticed, for instance, that you filed my notes on quinine substitutes in the wrong drawer," he smiled at her over a row of test tubes, "and you forgot to bring me the drugs I requisitioned for tomorrow's experiment."

Cherry pressed her hands against her tingling face. "I'm sorry. If you'll give me your authorization, I'll get the drugs right away. I'm not much help to you, am I, Dr. Joe?"

"We-ell, I really need a technical assistant. But I'm going to keep you on for company. After all, if your mother has Midge, then I ought to have her daughter in exchange. That's only fair, isn't it?" He pottered around the long laboratory sink. "About the assistant——"

Dr. Joe fumbled in the pocket of his crumpled laboratory coat. Cherry waited for him to finish his remark. He took some notes out of his pocket, searched for a pencil, sat down on a stool, and absorbedly started to write. Cherry was used to this.

In two or three minutes, he looked up again and grinned sheepishly. "Where were we?"

"About a technician for you," Cherry prompted.

Dr. Fortune rose from the stool and seated himself slowly in the one comfortable chair. "He looks old," Cherry thought, "and tired. It's no wonder, the way he drives himself with this research." Aloud she said, "Couldn't you take a little vacation, Dr. Joe? Perhaps around Thanksgiving? Midge will have vacation from high school that week end."

"Vacation! With our hospitals desperately understaffed? Does malaria, or the other tropical diseases, take a vacation? Do our soldiers in the Pacific get vacations from danger and infection?" Then he said less sternly, "I think I've found the man I want."

"Who is it?" Cherry asked.

"He came to me voluntarily because he, too, is interested in research for developing quinine substitutes. He says he's not a specialist in it, but he knows the field like a specialist." Dr. Fortune tamped down the tobacco in his pipe, thinking aloud as he often did with Cherry. "This staff man can give me only a little of his crowded time. A technician could give me his full time—if there were a technician to spare in wartime!" He talked a little further about the man's abilities and the technical aspects of the research.

Cherry found it difficult to understand and she involuntarily glanced down at her watch. There was not much time to get Dr. Joe his supplies before the main laboratory in Spencer was locked for the day. She rose. Where *did* time go? She ought to spend some time with her probie, she wanted to have time for Lex——

"Would you stop in at the office," Dr. Joe was saying, "and ask them to have Dr. Upham come in and see me?"

"Who?" Cherry asked, startled.

"Lex Upham, the man I was telling you about." Dr. Joe patted her cheek. "You'll have to meet him."

Cherry said meekly, "That's right, I will meet him here, won't I?"

So he wasn't just a fly-by-night! She had supposed he was joking about becoming Dr. Joe's assistant. From now on, she would approach Dr. Lex Upham with the same respect and caution as a stick of dynamite. It occurred to her, with a grin, that coming to Dr. Joe's laboratory would be even nicer when Lex started his work here next month.

It was not until several busy days later that Cherry met Lex himself. He happened to be, or he said he "just happened to be," passing through the Obstetrics Clinic, when Cherry went off duty at three. She rushed up to him, noticing that he looked very much amused about something.

"How'd you do it?" she demanded, not bothering with preliminaries.

"I told you I would," he replied with a grin.

"But you're not a specialist in——"

"I became one. I spent every night last week until four A.M. reading every book I could find in this city on the subject." His golden brown eyes twinkled. "I read it so I could qualify to work with Dr. Fortune so he'd invite me to his lab so I could see you. It's simple."

Cherry had never before thought of sitting up all night reading books on quinine substitutes as a romantic gesture. But that was what it was. There was something irresistibly funny about such a direct and studious approach, and something touching too. Cherry's expression was a very puzzled one.

"I know what you're thinking," Lex said as he shoved open the door into the yard for her. "But, believe it or not, I have a lighter side. For instance, I'm a wonderful dancer. I could prove it if you'd have dinner with me tonight." He strode along, smiling at her, his sand-colored hair ruffled by the tangy October wind. "Well? Well? Are you still intimidated by a few rules?"

Cherry turned a laughing face to him. "Lex, honestly you do deserve something in return for all that studying, and for all the extra work you'll do with Dr. Joe."

"That's all right," he interrupted. "The more I read, the more interested I got. I'm keen on doing that research for its own sake now."

"So I don't count any more!" Cherry teased.

"Certainly you count and don't say such idiotic things," he commanded. "If you're going to twist my remarks——"

"If you can't take a little teasing——"

They both broke off short, and faced each other in a flare-up of anger. Suddenly Cherry started to laugh. "We certainly are two of a kind!" She took out her white handkerchief and waved it. "Truce! Truce!"

"Truce declared." He took her arm, smiling again. "Now about some dancing——"

"Quiet, you rebel! You know I can't afford to break the rules."

He jammed his hands into his pockets. "No, I suppose you can't. Well, there's a dance here at the hospital way off next week. That's legal."

"Is that an invitation?" Cherry teased, though she knew she should not provoke his lightning temper.

He bowed from the waist. "I will have it engraved, Madame." He straightened up and looked her full in the eyes. "You adopted me and that includes the dance."

Cherry retreated into Crowley. She remembered a line from an old popular song, "You may have been a headache, but you never were a bore. . . ."

"Anyway, I'll have free time for the dance," Cherry consoled herself, as she got out her books to study. She would like to see Ann and Gwen other than just at mealtime but they were both now on relief duty, from three P.M. to eleven P.M., when she was off. All the seniors were rushing like plagued creatures. "A dance will be a nice break for us poor seniors. I'll count off the days against that." And Cherry determinedly opened her book, to study for Delivery Room work which was almost upon her.

It was still six days before the dance, when Cherry had a meeting with her other adoptee, Mildred Burnham.

With Mildred on her conscience, Cherry had left three notes in the girl's room trying to make an appointment. The first two had gone unanswered. But here the two girls were, finally, on a Sunday afternoon in the deserted lounge.

Outside, the wind rustled the red and gold leaves, and the sky was very blue. Cherry longed to be outdoors, but Mildred did not want to go for a walk. She sat slouched in a chair, her lumpy face wearing its habitual sullen expression. Cherry settled herself resignedly in her own chair and sighed. She felt as if she were pulling, all alone, on a heavy weight. After some preliminary small talk, she made a start.

"It's only a little over a month until probationers are capped, Mildred——"

"——or expelled," the girl interrupted. "You don't have to worry about me."

"I'm not worried, because I'm sure you're doing very nice work." Cherry tried to smooth the girl's prickly feelings. "But every one of us has her weak points and I wondered if you might want some special coaching."

"No, thanks."

Cherry felt as if she were pushing against a wall. Wasn't there a door anywhere in this closed wall? She talked for a while about what the probationers' written and oral and practical examinations would be like.

Mildred listened but made no response. Recalling her own probie experience, Cherry warned Mildred what an ordeal capping could be and suggested how she might best face it. There was no response to this, either. At last Cherry said:

"I wish we could be friends, Mildred. I'd like to be. Wouldn't you?"

Mildred Burnham gave her a sharp look. "You don't feel friendly toward me."

Cherry felt caught up short. It was true she did not like Mildred. So the girl sensed it! "You're rather difficult to be friends with," Cherry reminded her gently.

"Then why don't you let it go?" Mildred said, getting to her feet. And Cherry was too discouraged, after this awful half-hour, to push the interview further. She wondered how in the world she was going to deal with Mildred Burnham for a whole year.

A few days later, a talk she had with Bertha Larsen did not help matters. Cherry had learned that Mildred was on the same ward with Bertha, and she asked the good-humored farm girl how Mildred's ward work was going.

"Well," said Bertha and stopped, troubled. "Mildred's work is all right, but she does not understand that we all must work together. She is a little selfish—" Bertha stopped again. "Maybe she just tries too hard," she said apologetically.

"You mean she grabs the best of everything for her own patients and leaves the rest of you to get along as you can?" Cherry asked sharply.

"Sometimes," Bertha admitted. "She hurries and takes hers, as if she did not trust the rest of us. Oh, it's nothing! She's just a foolish little probie, she will get over it."

Cherry made a point of seeing Mildred Burnham that same afternoon. She came straight to the subject of the way Mildred was behaving on the ward. Cherry was angry that Bertha Larsen, who was so kind-hearted and generous, should be imposed upon. She felt it was hopeless to try to be friendly or kind or understanding with Mildred. So she spoke sharply to her probationer, to drive her point home.

Mildred looked unhappy. It was the first time Cherry had seen any expression except sullenness on the girl's face.

"I'm sorry to scold you," Cherry said, picking up her cape to leave. "But it's better to hear this from your adopting senior than from your head nurse—or from Training School Office."

"You don't like me," said Mildred Burnham accusingly.

There it was again! Cherry flung her nurse's cape about her shoulders and hurried out into the rotunda, feeling almost guilty. She was troubled for several days, and even more troubled when Miss Reamer routinely called her to her office.

"How are you and Miss Burnham getting on?" the Superintendent of Nurses asked.

Cherry looked at the floor. "We're not. Perhaps it's my fault."

"You are a little impatient, you know, Miss Ames. I want a more cheerful report next time—if you are to go on being a guiding senior." Miss Reamer smiled and the talk turned to Cherry's studies. But the worry about Mildred Burnham stuck in Cherry's mind.

The day of the dance, when it finally came, was one long disappointment for Cherry. She worked an extremely hard eight hours on the mothers' ward, until her head felt like a balloon and her feet seemed to weigh ten pounds each. After that Dr. Joe, in all innocence, asked her to run errands. Cherry barely made second supper and choked down her food. Then she headed frantically for lecture class. On the way, a phone call came from Obstetrical. The relief nurse was sick this evening: the hospital was short of nurses since so many had gone off to the battlefronts: would Miss Ames take over the ward in this emergency until eleven P.M.? She would, of course. Cherry went back to the ward and resumed her duties. Her whole body ached with fatigue. But hearing music drift faint and tantalizing across the yard was the worst of it. The dance had started. And Cherry had missed it—after all that waiting.

"I don't care," Cherry pretended as she walked softly around the sleeping ward with her flashlight. "Who cares about a dance, anyhow, even if it *is* the first senior dance?"

Her disappointment grew sharper when at eleven o'clock the night nurse came to relieve her. Cherry went downstairs and stood alone in the deserted clinic. She was tired and dirty and the distant music sounded very sweet.

"Cherry!" someone hissed.

Cherry whirled around. It was Lex. He walked toward her smiling, offered her an arm, swung her into dancing position, and they were smoothly fox trotting past the examination booths.

"Lex, you idiot—what——"

"The music's good tonight, isn't it?" he smiled down at her. He executed a double step, off-beat, and guided her skilfully past an interviewer's deserted desk. "Are you enjoying the dance, Miss Ames?"

Cherry began to smile. "Yes, Dr. Upham, the music *is* good tonight."

The distant music stopped for a moment. Lex and Cherry both gravely applauded. Then a waltz started far away, and they waltzed up and down between the long rows of empty clinic benches.

"May I have the next dance?" Lex inquired as the music stopped again.

"But what about my other partners?" Cherry giggled back.

"I won't permit any cutting-in," Lex said. A faint fox trot started, and they danced to it, their shoes sounding loud in the deserted clinic.

"You're really a good dancer," Cherry said.

"Thanks." He whirled her past an instrument case. They smiled at each other as they turned and dipped.

"In fact," Cherry said contentedly, "this is a pretty nice dance!"

~~~~~~

CHAPTER V

Midge Makes Mischief

A TYPEWRITTEN NOTICE WAS TACKED ON THE BULLETIN board, on the cold morning of November first:

> Ames, C. . . . . Delivery Room
> Jones, G. . . . . Delivery Room

That plunged Cherry into a thoroughly alien world. But having Gwen with her was cheering. Ann was going, temporarily, to the next-door Children's Clinic where they were shorthanded.

"Welcome to our next hurdle," Cherry greeted the redhead on their first morning together. They were walking down the short, silent, empty corridors of Obstetrical Ward. "This ward is a humdinger. This is where they make or break seniors."

"It looks innocent enough," Gwen objected. "There's not a sight or sound within miles. I've never been any place so peaceful—on the surface. Look, what's this?"

Both girls stopped to peek in at a small room. It was the first of a series of rooms, a little like Operating Rooms with everything kept sterile but less completely equipped. Cherry's eye fell on a baby's scale. "Couldn't you guess?"

"Delivery Room, where the newest generation arrives, and I win the wooden umbrella," Gwen said triumphantly.

"You nut!" Cherry giggled. "But it'll be nice having you and your monkey business around again."

Gwen poked her red head inquisitively into one of the empty private rooms. "It's going to be nice, too, to have regular hours again, after all that relief duty," she replied.

They were both wrong. They were to see very little of one another here, and hours turned out to be wildly irregular. For the expected babies paid no attention to hospital schedules.

When the girls reported to the head nurse in charge, they understood why this ward was the seniors' Big Worry. Miss Sprague was an ageless woman with an iron face and old, pioneer attitudes. She had nursed for years, often under conditions that would have intimidated even Daniel Boone. Miss Sprague thought that any nurse with less than twenty years' experience was unreliable ("though how are we to *get* experience in the first place?" Cherry asked Gwen) and she referred quite openly to her student nurses as "those young snips." Miss Sprague, with her tall spare figure, ramrod posture and tightly knotted hair, was permanently disgusted with youth. She was famous for sending in severe reports on her student nurses. Several seniors had been flunked out on the basis of Miss Sprague's reports on them.

"As a matter of fact," Cherry confided to Gwen, after they had introduced themselves to the head nurse and had been morally trampled into their places, "she *might* be right. Assisting at childbirth is delicate work and I for one am a little nervous about it."

"There's nothing to be nervous about," Gwen said sturdily. "After all, it's traditionally women's work. Way back, before we had hospitals or even many doctors in this country, midwives delivered *all* babies. My father says that even now midwives supervise about fifteen per cent of the births here—and heaven knows how much bigger per cent in other countries. So there."

"But it's a far cry from a midwife to a trained obstetrician, and a trained obstetrical nurse," Cherry replied. "You just can't compare them. The difference shows in how many mothers and babies live or die in the process of getting babies born."

"Absolutely," Gwen agreed. Her eyes suddenly opened wide. "Gosh, it's pretty important stuff, isn't it? Hmm. I don't feel so nonchalant now myself."

Cherry started to laugh. She thought of Miss Sprague and her laughter died.

Cherry's first case started out easily enough. Young Mrs. Reed was admitted to the hospital in the afternoon, just a few hours before Cherry was to go off duty. Cherry stayed on, because of the possible "rush element." Mrs. Reed's baby might put in its appearance quite suddenly, and everybody would spring into instant action. On the other hand, Mrs. Reed's baby might dawdle. Cherry wished the baby would come promptly.

Mrs. Reed was a humorous, pretty young woman. She strolled in joking and brushing off her hovering mother and her distracted young husband. "Nurse, please tell them to stop fussing and mourning so," she asked Cherry. "Producing future citizens is a perfectly healthy, normal process."

"Suppose she has twins," young Mr. Reed groaned.

"Nurse, I must tell you," Mrs. Reed's stout and bossy mother pushed forward importantly. "My daughter Diana has always been very nervous, and this is her first baby, you simply must not let her——"

"I'll be outside your door all night," young Mr. Reed said dolefully.

Cherry said reassuring things, got her patient into the little private room, and closed the door on the other two. In her amusement, Cherry lost a little of her own nervousness.

"They mean so well," young Mrs. Reed grinned at Cherry, "and they make such nuisances of themselves. But they do scare me a little," she admitted.

"Here, here, none of that," Cherry replied. "Who's scared?"

She helped Mrs. Reed into bed, gave her a warm relaxing sponge bath, and watched constantly for any signs of complications. Cherry knew all this in theory, but this was her first actual practice, and she wanted to give her patient the best of care. It heartened her to have Miss Sprague come in and check up and say that Cherry had done everything all right. "So far," the head nurse added ominously.

Later the house doctor and one of the floor nurses came in, too, to check up and to give Cherry a rest period. Baby Reed was still somewhere in the offing. Cherry gave Mrs. Reed her supper and several times cheered up Mr. Reed in the hall. The evening rather tensely wore on.

"They say first babies are usually awfully slow in coming," young Mrs. Reed fretted. "My mother warned me—Oh, she's probably full of old wives' tales. Just the same, Miss Ames, I'm upset."

Cherry talked to her and encouraged her.

"Don't go away, Nurse."

"I won't."

Much later, Mrs. Reed said, "Would you—would you see if my husband is still out there? And if he is, please send the poor man home." Cherry admired her when she added with a laugh, "Poor Dick! He's taking this much harder than I am. He's the one to worry about, not me."

Cherry barely had opened the door into the corridor when Mr. Reed sprang up from a bench. His face was pale and drawn. His tie had come unknotted and his hair was rumpled.

"How is she? How is she? Has the baby come? Isn't there something I can *do?*"

Cherry felt sorry for him, but she had a hard time keeping a straight face. "Your wife is fine and the baby won't be here for ages. Why don't you——"

But he would not go home. He clung to Cherry's apron desperately, pleadingly. Cherry's heart went out to him. He looked so much like a bewildered, frightened little boy. Suddenly Cherry had an inspiration. "Something to do, that's it. Make him feel he's helping."

"Why don't you go to that lovely little florist shop on the corner—they stay open quite late—and surprise Mrs. Reed with her favorite flowers. She'd love them, wouldn't she? And besides, she'd feel that she's a lucky wife to have such a thoughtful husband."

Satisfied at last that he could do something, the young husband dashed off. Cherry, with a happy smile, closed the door on his retreating figure and went back to waiting. She turned her patient in the bed to a more comfortable position, bathed her hands and face, and gave her a back massage, and then some light nourishment. It was a long wait. Still, everything seemed to be going all right, to Cherry's relief. The night deepened. Mrs. Reed talked, vaguely and emotionally at times, confiding to Cherry things she never would have told except under stress.

"What a lot a nurse learns about people," Cherry thought, as she held the young woman's hand there in the half-dark, "and what a lot of secrets she must keep!"

A long time later, Mrs. Reed's voice came softly:

"Nurse. I'm glad you're here with me."

"I'm not really doing much for you," Cherry replied honestly.

"You're *there*. That's everything."

Cherry thought of something she had learned early in her first year and had never forgotten: a nurse has to care for people's minds and hearts, as well as their physical ills. Her worries, her fatigue dropped away. She felt refreshed and rewarded. Let Miss Sprague flunk her if she wanted to! Miss Sprague could not take away this moment, or her patient's gratitude, from her, ever.

Presently Cherry realized it was time to call the supervisor—or was it time? She sprang to her feet, jerked on the lights and excitedly tried to decide whether this was the moment to notify Miss Sprague to summon the obstetrician. She dare not delay. Yet in her inexperience she must not take the obstetrician away from other urgent cases any sooner than he was needed here. Cherry tried desperately to remember the text-book page which danced mockingly before her eyes. Oh, why hadn't she studied this until it was second nature? Better not take any chances! She rang for the first-year nurse and sent the girl to notify the head nurse. Meanwhile, with the aid of an orderly, Cherry hastily got Mrs. Reed onto a stretcher. They hurried into the small shining white room and, even in her excitement, Cherry stopped short in surprise.

The obstetrician, Dr. Walker, that immaculate figure in white, was a woman.

Somehow it seemed to Cherry an appropriate and sympathetic arrangement. Cherry scrubbed up as fast as she could, feeling pleased. She was pleased when Dr. Walker held out slim capable hands for Cherry to slip on sterile rubber gloves, and bent an attractive sleek head for Cherry to tie on the gauze cap and face mask.

From then on, Dr. Walker was very businesslike and very busy. Cherry was alert and quick to anticipate the doctor's every move. She wondered anxiously whether Dr. Walker was satisfied with the way she assisted. But she was too thrilled to think of anything but the baby.

The sun and the baby arrived at the same moment. He was brick red, wrinkled and wiry—he looked like nothing human. Dr. Walker was laughing and holding him high by his heels.

"You have a fine boy!" she told Mrs. Reed. And she spanked him hard to start him breathing. Cherry winced when the doctor walloped him, but she knew it was necessary. The baby let out a yell.

Mrs. Reed woke for a moment. "Is it—you said it's a boy?" she whispered.

"Yes, a boy," Cherry told her. "You have a son."

Dr. Walker held the squirming baby up for Mrs. Reed to see. The young woman's eyes were fastened wonderingly on him. And the expression on her face moved Cherry very much. "My baby," she breathed. "Tell Dick," she murmured to Cherry and was asleep.

"He's a nice baby," the obstetrician said with satisfaction, handing the baby to Cherry.

"Yes, he's a nice baby," Cherry thought happily as she wrapped him in a warm blanket and weighed him. "And my patient's all right and I got through my first taste of this without mishap. Thank heavens!" She began to feel tired, now that the night's excitement which had buoyed her up was over.

But Cherry was not quite finished. At the doctor's crisp direction, Cherry treated the baby's eyes with one per cent silver nitrate, to prevent infection which might lead to blindness. Then she sealed his bead name bracelet on his tiny wrist. Finally she put him, on his right side, in a special, warmed bed. A nursery nurse came for the baby. Cherry wished Dr. Walker would give her a word of approbation, even make a comment of any kind. But the obstetrician was already dashing out of the door.

Out in the corridor, Cherry told two orderlies to which room to take Mrs. Reed, and started to think of a warm drink, and her nice soft bed. Suddenly, out of nowhere, young Mr. Reed sprang at her again. This time his hair was standing straight on end, the buttons on his coat were dangling by their threads, and he was hanging on for dear life to a big basket of flowers. He made such a comical figure that Cherry's fatigue and misgivings evaporated in an overwhelming desire to laugh.

"Nurse! Is she all right?"

"Oh, you poor man!" Cherry thought, choking back her laughter. She said as convincingly as she could, "Your wife is fine, just fine."

"I mean Mrs. Reed! The little one with the dark hair! Is *she*——"

Cherry nodded. "Mrs. Reed, the little one with the dark hair, is just fine. You can see her soon."

The disheveled young man sank down onto a bench in the hall. "Whew!"

"Incidentally," Cherry reminded him, and her dark eyes danced, "you have a son." She felt a little proud, as if she were partly responsible for Baby Reed.

"A—a what?"

"A son."

"Oh, is that so?" he responded politely. It had not registered.

"A son. A boy," Cherry tried again.

He looked completely dazed. Cherry brought him some coffee, and started to go off duty at long last. But Mr. Reed darted after her and thrust the great basket of flowers at Cherry.

"You were wonderful to my wife. She would want you to have these flowers," he babbled. "We want to show our appreciation!"

At precisely that moment Miss Sprague passed by. She sized up the situation with cold eyes that told nothing. Cherry could just imagine the head nurse snorting, "It's a pity you aren't as good as those flustered patients think you are!"

Mr. Reed was urging the flowers on her. "You *do* like flowers! Didn't I hear you say so?" he asked in full earshot of Miss Sprague. "I know we owe you a lot," he gulped.

Cherry trembled in embarrassment and exasperation. Mr. Reed meant well, but he was downright dangerous. "You don't owe me anything. I only did my job," Cherry said loudly and prayed that Miss Sprague had heard.

"I can't accept anything, though it's very kind of you." She fled.

It was not easy, after that incident, to go directly into the head nurse's office to report off duty.

"Well!" The dour head nurse's eyes traveled over Cherry's tired face and figure. "Straighten up, Miss Ames. You needn't sag as though you'd been through anything difficult last night. The case you had was perfectly simple. Luckily for you."

"Yes, Miss Sprague," Cherry murmured. She was too weary to protest, and she could not afford to antagonize her head nurse, anyway.

Miss Sprague bent stiffly forward. "Did I hear that man say you had hinted for a gift?"

"But what he said wasn't——"

"Miss Ames, I will not tolerate my nurses 'working' the patients for gifts or tips! It is downright dishonest! A nurse's first concern is her patient, not herself!"

"But I didn't—" Cherry gasped out in dismay.

"That will do, Miss Ames. I heard what he said! You will give your patients decent care without expecting any gratuities. Do you understand me?"

Cherry sighed. "Yes, Miss Sprague."

She understood. She understood only too well that the head nurse had gotten a false and vicious idea about her into her stubborn head. Cherry signed out and walked away wretchedly.

Cherry worked on Delivery Room for a month without ever having any further inkling of what the head nurse thought of her or of her work. Gwen, too, on the rare occasions and crazy hours when Cherry saw her, was equally puzzled and anxious. Dr. Walker dropped a kind word occasionally, but doctors did not report on student nurses. Cases came and cases went. With the new mothers came frantic husbands and assorted relatives. Cherry learned a great deal about people, as well as about nursing, in that month. But she never learned what the terrible Miss Sprague thought of her total performance.

Only one thing was clear. Since that little flower scene with Mr. Reed, the head nurse seemed to dislike Cherry.

"It's discouraging," she murmured to Gwen in the supply closet, the day before Thanksgiving. "I'm in wrong with Miss Sprague, anyhow, so no matter what else I do now, good or bad, it can't make any difference. And I'm just about ready to burst."

That was why, when Midge stuck her merry face in the door of an empty private room that afternoon, Cherry broke loose.

"Midge!" Cherry felt a rush of warmth at seeing someone she really cared about on this friendless ward. She dropped the linens of the bed she was remaking and hugged Midge. "Of all the gorgeous surprises! How come?"

"Thanksgiving week end, high school's closed!" Midge hugged her back.

"Look at the girl!" Cherry declared. "She's going to be a beauty!"

Midge stood up proudly for Cherry's inspection. She was a healthy, glowing girl, quick and light in her movements. Her face, with its shining eyes, tilted nose, and wide shapely mouth, seemed always to be laughing. Her thick light-brown hair cascaded over the shoulders of her boyish gray woolen coat.

"Let's see what color your eyes are today," Cherry laughed and swung Midge toward the window.

The color of Midge's eyes was a standing joke, for they were always changing. Sometimes they appeared hazel, in summer they were almost green, at night velvety brown. Today they seemed gray, because she was wearing gray. They were very clear, candid eyes.

"Now that we have that problem settled," Midge said, "how are you? I want to know dozens of things! Can you come out with me?"

"Have you abandoned your wild ways, now that you've reached the ripe old age of fifteen? Is it safe for me to go out with you?" Cherry countered. Then she laughed. "I'm reporting off this very minute! Wait in the hall for me."

Out in the hall, they raced toward the stairs. Midge had already started down, when someone imperiously called Cherry. It was Lex.

Dr. Upham was in a great hurry and in a bad temper, "I've been trying for days to see you alone," he said "Look here, Cherry, would you——"

Just then Midge turned back and joined their twosome. Lex looked annoyed.

"This is Midge Fortune," Cherry said out of the awkward pause.

"Midge, huh? She looks like a midge," Lex said.

"Why, you meanie!" Cherry said warmly, "Midge is practically my little sister. It's high time you met her."

"Couldn't we meet some other day?" Lex said curtly. "Right now I want to talk to you alone about——"

"Lex, you're very rude!" Cherry's black eyes snapped. She could see that the younger girl felt snubbed and upset.

"I didn't want especially to meet you today, either," Midge said coolly.

Lex glared at the fifteen-year-old. Then he glared at Cherry. Ignoring Midge, he said to Cherry, "I'll see you some other time when you're unencumbered, and when you're feeling a little more reasonable!" He turned on his heel and strode away.

Midge looked after him with her face quite red. "So that's your sweetheart! If he thinks he can talk that way to me——!"

"I never told you he was my sweetheart! He's not, he's just a friend," Cherry said hastily. "And he didn't mean to be rude. He's just rather abrupt." Yet she felt sorry that Midge had been hurt.

"Well, I don't like being snubbed!" Midge tossed her head. "I'll teach him! I know. I'll send him something funny that'll make him mad!"

"Midge, he's a staff doctor, you mustn't——"

Midge's young face was crinkling with laughter. "Let's go downtown and buy a box of lollipops to sweeten him up!"

Cherry felt herself weakening. She sympathized with Midge about Lex's snub—and she never could resist playing a joke. "A box of lollipops to match his childish behavior," she agreed dryly.

"And we'll put a funny note in it!" Midge went on. "I'll write it while you're dressing."

They raced back to Crowley and Cherry's room. While Cherry slipped into street clothes, Midge took paper, envelope, and a pen from Cherry's desk.

"What'll we say?" Midge poised the pen above the paper. She remembered that she was furious. "Something that will fix him!"

Just then a nurse rapped on Cherry's door. The ward was telephoning her on some routine question. Cherry sped out of the room, leaving Midge alone.

When she returned, Midge was just sealing the envelope.

"What did you write?" Cherry asked, grinning.

"Oh, just a joke," Midge assured her airily and pounded down the flap.

Something in her face made Cherry suspicious. "You didn't write anything you shouldn't have? You aren't trying to meddle or be smart, are you?"

"Certainly not!" Midge was properly indignant. "How could I? You've never told me anything much about Lex. I heard about him only from Dad."

"And I won't tell you anything, because there isn't anything to tell. And it's not for little pitchers with big ears, anyway."

"Yes, Grandma," Midge said. "Now hurry up, or the stores will be closed!"

They bought the box of lollipops and carefully sent it not to Lex's residence, but to Dr. Joe's office—"so Dad can get a laugh out of it, too," Midge said. She and Cherry had tucked Midge's note firmly in with the candy.

If Cherry could have seen what was inside the sealed envelope, she would never have sent it. For Midge had written:

Dear Dr. Upham:

As Cherry's oldest friend, I happen to know quite a few things about you. I know she did not like your impolite behavior to me in the hall. It is too bad I cannot divulge her confidences, and tell you a number of other things she does not like about you, besides. If you and Cherry are really sweethearts, I'd advise you to mend your ways. Perhaps these lollipops, which we bought specially for you, will help sweeten your disposition. I do hope so—for Cherry's sake.

Yours sincerely,

Margaret Fortune

P. S. I am writing this because I want to see Cherry happy.

Dr. Joe was so annoyed over a seemingly innocent box of lollipops that he sent Midge home at once. Lex avoided Cherry and when she came to Dr. Joe's laboratory, he stormed out. She could not guess that Lex thought she had talked to Midge out of turn. Cherry was puzzled, then angry. Worst of all, Dr. Joe was so cold and aloof that Cherry stayed away from the lab for a couple of weeks. She was so distracted that she earned herself additional scoldings from Miss Sprague. The rest of the month on Delivery Room was very gloomy indeed.

On the final day, Cherry and Gwen steeled themselves. They waited until no one was in the corridor, then crept up to the bulletin board. They read, then looked at each other disbelievingly.

"Has a miracle happened?" Cherry breathed. "Look— we're being sent on to another ward. That must mean we've passed Delivery Room!"

Gwen wrung her hands together thankfully. "We're actually out of Sprague's clutches at last!"

The typewritten notice tacked on the bulletin board was dated December first and read:

Ames, C. . . . . Nursery

Jones, G. . . . . Nursery

CHAPTER VI

~~~~~~

An Orchid or Gardenias

CHERRY HEARD IT FROM SOMEONE ELSE. SHE WAS GLAD AND relieved, yet at the same time she felt curiously left out.

Mildred Burnham had won her nurse's cap. Cherry's adoptee had successfully completed her probationary period and was now a full-fledged student nurse. Bertha Larsen told Cherry on the day of capping, and then some of her other classmates congratulated Cherry. But Mildred herself never said a word to Cherry about it, never even came near her.

"Maybe she doesn't want my congratulations," Cherry reminded herself, recalling the girl's defensive attitude, "but I'm going to tell her, anyway, that I think she deserves a lot of credit!"

As soon as she could get off her own ward, Cherry raced over to Mildred's ward. But Mildred had gone off duty half an hour before, the head nurse said. Cherry went on over to the first-year and junior students' residence hall. Mildred was not in her room. Cherry left a note.

"Good for you!" she scribbled. "I know you did it all by yourself." She frowned at that: would Mildred think that she was angry because her help had been refused? Cherry took another piece of paper. "I know from my own experience that winning one's cap isn't easy." Cherry's pencil hesitated above the paper. She wanted to write, quite sincerely, "I'm proud for you. I know you'll win your graduate's ribbon too." But would Mildred imagine some patronizing overtone? Rather self-consciously, Cherry curbed her enthusiasm and finished the note. She folded it and pushed it all the way under Mildred's door. She hoped Mildred would reply.

Mildred did not reply that day, nor the day after capping. All the other seniors and their ex-probies were celebrating. Cherry put down her own adoptee's snub to Mildred's mixed-up, immature emotions, and went over to Mildred's room again.

Mildred came to the door, with her new cap framing her heavy, expressionless face. She did not ask Cherry to come in. Cherry stood in the corridor feeling unwelcome and awkward. Perhaps, she thought, this ill-at-ease girl felt even more awkward than she did.

"It's grand, Mildred," Cherry said with an effort. "The cap certainly looks natural on you. Now you're really on your way to nursing!"

Mildred studied her with suspicious eyes. "I'll bet you're surprised I got it." Her voice implied, "You're sorry I got it."

Cherry was stunned. Then she tossed back her black curls and managed to laugh. "Don't say that! I'm glad, really glad for you. And I'm proud to have 'my' probie a success. Come on out and celebrate," Cherry invited.

"No."

Cherry's crimson cheeks burned as if Mildred had slapped her. The younger girl stood there—inert, hostile, almost boorish. Yet Cherry sensed that if she had not come to congratulate Mildred, Mildred would have felt neglected. Mildred seemed to need and want affection, yet was unable to accept it. How was she to get through the year with this strange and difficult girl? Why, what was she to say next?

But Mildred spoke next. "I have to go back to my studies," she said, with a curious expression. "Good-by." Mildred's door closed in her face.

A flash of resentment went through Cherry. She warned herself again not to be intolerant, but she felt unpleasantly shaken. She stared at the closed door. "Well, that is most certainly that," she thought. And from that moment, and for a long time afterwards,

Cherry disgustedly and deliberately turned her attention away from Mildred Burnham.

But Mildred Burnham remained a troubling, insistent problem in the back of Cherry's mind. The problem was deferred, not solved. Miss Reamer supervised Cherry in her role of Adopting Senior. Cherry talked to her twice about her troubles with Mildred. Miss Reamer made it clear that Cherry was lacking in understanding and patience. "Try to really like your adoptee," she counseled. Cherry wanted to, but she could not.

The first day it snowed, Cherry met young Dr. Lex Upham in the yard. It was a real snowstorm, with the white flakes coming so thick and fast that Cherry, bundled up in a big coat and her head bent, collided with his big solid figure. She would have slipped except for his instant strong grip on her arm.

"We always meet violently, don't we?" he laughed and peered at her through the whirling flakes. Cherry's black hair was dotted with white, her cheeks were brilliant, her eyes shone.

"Don't you love this weather?" she gasped. "Where's your hat?" His sandy hair was covered with snow.

"In Dr. Fortune's laboratory," he said, tucking her arm firmly under his. "After all my trouble to get myself in there, why don't you——"

"I'm in disgrace," she replied. "I thought you——"

"No, I'm not mad at you," Lex guessed before she could finish her remark. Neither of them referred to the lollipop incident; they were too glad to see each other. A gust of wind and snow blew in their faces. "How about some hot tea?" he shouted over the wind. With his lordly stride, he led her along toward Spencer Hall. "There's that sissy tearoom———"

"The rules say no! You'll get me into trouble yet!"

Lex flung open the door to Spencer rotunda and they were suddenly out of the wind and cold. It was warm and quiet here.

"Well, good-by, Miss Ames. It was nice seeing you." His golden brown eyes, under their sharp black brows, twinkled. He strode off, then abruptly turned. "By the way, I'm taking you to the doctors' Christmas Eve dance."

"You might ask me if—" she started, but he called back:

"Make up your mind whether you want an orchid or gardenias." Then he vigorously marched around the corner.

Cherry shrugged. Who could stay angry with a boy like that? She brushed the snow off her shoulders and sauntered into the lounge. She did not see Ann and Gwen walking slowly behind her, shaking their heads and smiling.

That evening, in lecture class, Gwen slid a note across the wide arm of her chair. Cherry opened it, and jumped. "An orchid or gardenias?" it inquired. Under that, Gwen had written, "Brave girl!"

Cherry forgot the lecture and wrote back indignantly, "He's *nice*."

Gwen nodded her head in total disbelief. Ann, who had been reading this correspondence over their shoulders, gave Cherry a quick nudge which Cherry hastily passed on to Gwen; the lecturer was frowning at them. Presently Ann, too, shoved over a note: "Is he as brilliant as they say? Is he human?" Cherry nodded twice in reply and then decided she had better pay attention to the lecture.

Senior subjects were difficult. Cherry thought back to her junior year, last year, and laughed at herself. She had worked, then, on Eye and Ear; on Skin (which she had missed in her first year because of an early vacation); on Private Pavilion and in several clinics. And she had thought *that* was hard!

When the lecture was over, not only Ann and Gwen but another half dozen girls pounced on Cherry with questions about Lex. "Of course we heard! How could we help hearing in the lounge?"—"I've been dying to ask you for weeks, you know perfectly well he's a sort of celebrity!"—" . . . and he proved to the senior surgeon that the instrument could really be improved and would you believe it, the senior surgeon retracted his statement!"—"He's terrifying! But he's not conceited.

You have to say that for him!"—"Well, if you think a cyclone is anything to play with. . . ."

"He is not strange!" Cherry tried to explain. She was so annoyed and so amused that she sputtered. "He's— he's perfectly human and awfully nice!"

They listened to her fairly enough. But no one could be convinced, despite Cherry's efforts, that Lex's fantastic reputation was what it was because of gossip long since wandered from the facts, plus fable, plus some dangerous envy. But they all respected Lex to the point of fear.

Cherry fell asleep that night wondering about Lex's fate here in the hospital, and trying to decide between gardenias and an orchid.

~~~~~~

CHAPTER VII

Double Trouble

SPENCER HOSPITAL WAS TINGLING WITH HOLIDAY excitement. It was still a good three weeks until Christmas, but already nurses were dragging fir trees to the wards and decorating them with the excited advice of their patients. Mysterious bundles were smuggled in and out of Crowley. Strange noises came from the basement of Spencer Hall where the doctors and internes were rehearsing for their Christmas Eve entertainment, to which they were inviting the seniors and graduates and other important members of the staff. Holly wreaths tied with wide red ribbons seemed to grow overnight in the lounge, the rotunda and the sleepy library. Out in the snow-laden yard, even the great white hospital buildings took on a festive look in the frosty air. Everyone hurried with a special lilt in his step, and the chef could not resist baking cakes iced with red and green instead of the usual white.

Cherry herself was pretty excited. Christmas meant not only Christmas to her, but her birthday as well. Cherry had always mourned that her birthday came the day before Christmas, with unfortunate effects on the gift situation. This year, though, she made it known that presents were taboo—except from her never-failing family, of course. Ann, Gwen, Bertha, Vivian, Josie, Marie and Mai Lee—all had loyally asked her what she wanted for her birthday.

"In wartime?" Cherry shook her head. They were all at supper together in the nurses' teeming dining room. "Thank you kindly and all that, but please skip it this year."

"I wasn't going to give you anything much," Gwen informed her. "Just one old shoe, say, or a lovely stick of stale chewing gum."

"We might take the same money and contribute it to some war fund where it's needed," Mai Lee suggested. The others looked at the quiet, slender, little Chinese-American girl. They knew Mai Lee was thinking of her family and her family's village, bombed to flame and dust. It was to avenge them, and to fight back effectively, that Mai Lee was becoming a nurse.

"We certainly might," Ann said. "And because it's Cherry's birthday, she can have the thankless job of treasurer. Don't bother to thank me, dear." She grinned at Cherry's gesture of despair. The purses promptly came out.

Bertha Larsen leaned forward. "There's something I ought to tell you—You don't expect presents, now honestly, do you? No, I don't think I'd better tell you after all." Her round pleasant face clouded as she seemed to be thinking of something.

"What's all this mystery?" Cherry puzzled, as she and Marie Swift together figured up the funds. "Two-fifty, three, and two more quarters here, Marie. . . . What were you trying to tell me, Bertha?"

But Bertha shook her head. There was no use trying to coax her, Cherry knew. Bertha was as stubborn as a mule sometimes.

"The seniors," Vivian announced, "are going down to the basement tonight."

Ann's face changed. "Oh, the basement! Yes," she said slowly.

There was indeed something to see in the vast basement under Spencer Hall. The Superintendent of Nurses herself assembled the senior class. She did not make any announcement. She merely asked them to follow her, and led them past the maze of service rooms to a further area of the basement. "Miss Reamer has a new hair-do," somebody whispered. But they had caught her serious mood and could not chatter tonight about her newly swirled gray locks. In the deepest part of the basement, Miss Reamer paused before a steel door. She unlocked it and switched on lights.

Here, far under the building, was a complete Operating Room! Beyond it, deep in shadow, they saw a great hall constructed with steel beams and thick brick walls. It was filled with at least a hundred cots. More cots, and stretchers, stood stacked against the walls. Adjoining it were a kitchen, bathrooms, a thoroughly stocked laboratory.

"Our country is at war," Miss Reamer said. "This new equipment is here in case of air raid or other catastrophe. I hope we will never have to use it."

Cherry felt her throat tighten. The young women's faces, under the blazing arc of the operating lamp, in the shadowy corners of the Operating Room, were soberly angry and determined. Miss Reamer locked the steel door and led them down a corridor along which were a series of small rooms. More cots, more stretchers, stood piled high on either side of the corridor. There was not much Christmas spirit down here. At intervals along the corridor new raw brick walls formed square safety zones.

Miss Reamer unlocked the door to one of the small rooms. "These are all alike," she said. Cherry and the others went in at Miss Reamer's invitation, and opened the tall steel lockers. They found heavy folded equipment for field hospitals. Ranged on the floor were dozens of black leather medical kits, containing supplies of all kinds.

"These things are yours," Miss Reamer said. "If it should ever be necessary, the seniors will ride ambulance with the doctors."

A murmur rose. It was a strange sort of Christmas present to the senior class.

"No one need go if she does not want to," Miss Reamer said gently.

The young women stirred. Their whispers surged around Cherry. "Of course we'll go!" the nurses were saying indignantly. "Try and stop us!" They looked expectantly toward the Superintendent of Nurses.

"What you see here is grim—but necessary," Miss Reamer went on. "Nurses above all people can face reality. I'm not worried about a single one of you— because I know you truly are nurses. And that's the highest praise I can give!"

Seeing the emergency equipment made Cherry restless. She was working this month on Nursery, with Gwen. Ordinarily, Cherry would have settled into this airy, peaceful ward as snugly as the babies slept in their little beds. There were no seasons here, no Christmas, no war.

Behind a glass partition, where proud parents and visitors could look in at them, lay a shelf of babies sleeping in a row. Each baby had a warm crib of his own, protected from draughts. Cherry was amused when the nurse in charge here told her to make these miniature, removable beds exactly as she would make a bed for adults, mitred corners and all. Another thing which amused Cherry, and touched her too, was to see big men doctors bending gently over tiny babies. There were nearly thirty babies here, brand-new from the Delivery Room, and all of them new acquaintances to Cherry. They kept Cherry and Gwen and the two graduates stepping.

"Feed one, and another one yowls for its whey," Gwen complained laughingly to Cherry. She had finished bathing one baby and was scrubbing up before touching another. Both girls were wearing gowns and masks over their mouths and noses, for babies are very susceptible to infection. "Feed that one and the first one howls again. It's a race!"

Cherry mumbled "Uh-huh" sympathetically but she was too busy to answer, what with the plump and wriggling baby on her lap. She had just washed his scalp with soap and water. But because he was less than ten days old, and his skin was so sensitive that it had turned bright red, she did not risk skin infection with a soap and water bath. Instead, Cherry gently cleansed him with a little oil. The baby seemed to be enjoying it, for he grunted and waved his arms and legs.

"What would you like to wear today?" she consulted the baby.

The baby blinked amiably but expressed no preference.

"In that case," Cherry lifted him up deftly, "what would you say to a square diaper, a nice cotton shirt and a fine old hospital gown?"

Apparently it was all right with the baby. Cherry thought it was something like playing dolls, but a good deal more satisfactory. She carried him back to his crib and put a loose light warm cover over him. He promptly fell asleep—"without so much as a thank you," Cherry thought, and went to scrub herself before bathing the next infant.

The moment she had turned her back on the shelf of babies, that restlessness again surged over her. Cherry did not know quite what it was. It seemed to have something to do with being a senior—restless at still being in school, impatient to work on her own as a professional.

"But taking care of new-born babies is important work," Gwen objected, when Cherry confided this to her. "Or maybe Christmas or facing a birthday does things to you. It does to me."

"It isn't either one—exactly—it's—Oh, I'm tired of being a mere student. I've acquired most of my skills by now. I want to get out in the world and use them."

"In just which part of the great wide world?" Gwen inquired practically. "And in just which branch of the dozens of branches of nursing?"

Cherry could not answer that, so she pretended to be busy at the formula table with nursing bottles, funnels, and kettles. "You win," she finally admitted meekly. "I don't know." Visions of those emergency kits rose before her eyes. "Yes, maybe I do know," she said suddenly. She could nurse right here on the home front—for civilians were fighting this war, too. But for a while, she would keep this half-decision to herself.

Gwen's bright inquisitive eyes warned Cherry a question was coming. Fortunately the lively young graduate nurse who was in charge of the premature babies came in just then.

"Hello, you two," she said with a pleasant nod. She had pinned a little sprig of holly on her uniform. "Miss Ames, we're sending Miss Jones another helper for today and you're coming in to help me. We're so short of special baby nurses that I'll have to take a chance on you."

Cherry's heart sank as she followed Miss Towne's brisk steps down the corridor. Handling normal babies was a delicate enough business, but caring for babies born at eight and a half months or earlier, or babies weighing less than five pounds at birth, was immeasurably more risky. Cherry's uneasiness grew as she entered the special room and the warm still air, kept always at eighty degrees, drowsily caressed her face. She and Miss Towne donned fresh masks.

"Too hot for you in here?" Miss Towne asked, seeing the red creep up Cherry's face above the gauze mask. "It's a bit uncomfortable until you get used to it. But you know, with these poor mites, loss of heat for even a little time can mean loss of life. See, each one has its heated incubator."

Cherry gazed down at the tiny, tiny babies, curled up asleep in their special beds, some of them not much bigger than her two fists. One of them had no fingernails or toenails yet. Another one had no eyelashes yet. It was work for them even to breathe. Miss Towne was saying they existed on breast milk, fed with a medicine dropper. Some of these morsels of humanity might live and some day become strong men and women, some might not survive the year. Cherry felt a wave of pity as she looked at the struggling little beings. She thought of their mothers, too.

"Would you—would you call this home-front nursing?" Cherry blurted out. The question sounded irrelevant. She could not say what had prompted her to ask it—this new restlessness, perhaps.

"How strange for you to say that!" Miss Towne exclaimed. "You must be reading my thoughts!" She looked searchingly at Cherry, then bit her lip.

"Why?"

Miss Towne looked embarrassed. "I hate to talk about it, and still, it's a relief to say it out loud. The Army's calling for nurses and I want to go. I'm young, I'm strong, and if I say so myself, I'm a good all-around nurse. I feel I ought to go. And to tell you the truth, Miss Ames," she smiled at Cherry, "I'm raring to get out of hospital routine and taste some excitement!

"But," Miss Towne looked pensively around at the babies in their incubators, "I ask myself what will become of these little creatures if I walk out on them. Someone has to save soldiers' lives. Someone has to save these infants' lives, too."

"The hospital will get a nurse to take your place," Cherry suggested.

"There isn't anybody to take my place. You see for yourself," Miss Towne said worriedly, "how all the young nurses are leaving here in droves for the Army hospitals. Why, our staff here is depleted!"

It was true. Cherry was pinch-hitting here right this minute, for that very reason. She remembered the extra nights she had put in on the wards a month and two months ago, because they were short-handed. Ann and Gwen had been pressed into service for extra hours, too. Suppose—on top of this shortage—suppose there were an emergency? Not necessarily an air raid: it might all too possibly be a train wreck, a flood, an epidemic. Where were the extra nurses to come from then?

Miss Towne set to work checking the babies' weight and they said no more about it. Cherry worked hard and with concentration all that day, but she could not get the question and the restlessness out of her mind. It shut out even the excitement of Christmas and her approaching birthday.

The Christmas gaiety was catching, though. In spite of herself, Cherry began to plan with Ann and Gwen what they would wear to the doctors' and internes' Christmas Eve entertainment. Dance dresses were permitted. It would be the first time Lex would see her in anything besides her work-a-day uniform.

Downtown, the city bustled with festive crowds and the shop windows glittered with holiday decorations. Cherry had glimpsed in one of the shops exactly the dress she would like to wear—if she only had it! It was a little sophisticated for her, she supposed, and definitely extravagant—the exquisite sort of dress which called for flowers in her hair and fragile high-heeled slippers and perfume and music. But there did not seem much hope of getting the dream dress, barring miracles. Cherry went about her work in the Nursery and tried, not too successfully, to forget about it. Before she knew it, her birthday was only two days off, Christmas Eve and the dance only three short days away. And she still had nothing to wear!

Cherry returned to her room that afternoon to find her family's birthday packages, and her father's letter and check, awaiting her. A check! Blessings on him! She obediently left the gifts unopened till her birthday, raced wildly downtown, found the dress still there and within reach of her purse, and practically floated on wings back to the hospital, hugging the lovely thing.

On her birthday—the day before Christmas— Cherry saved opening her presents until that afternoon, when Ann and Gwen and some of the others could be on hand. There were "Oh's" and "Ah's" as Cherry unwrapped the huge package from her mother: a warm gay red robe and furry slippers to match.

"You must have an awfully nice mother," Vivian Warren said wistfully. Vivian's mother, worn out by her long struggle with poverty, had too many children and too much work and worry to be able to show Vivian much affection.

"I have a darling mother," Cherry replied. She wished the girls could see her mother: a slender, sweet-faced woman, still youthful, interested and active, and with a sense of humor about everything, except her gardening.

Charlie's present was next, and as Cherry opened the box, she was startled. Her blond twin brother apparently had been unable to decide between a professional sort of gift and a very feminine gift, so with his usual devotion to Cherry, he had sent both. Side by side, Cherry found a shiny pair of bandage scissors and a bottle of perfume. He had written on the card, "One way or another, you'll slay 'em!"

"And what did your father send?" Ann asked, smiling.

"A check." Cherry glanced involuntarily toward the closet. "I spent it for that terrific dress I've been telling you about—you'll see it tonight." By now the dress had become a sort of symbol to her, a reward and an antidote for all this month's hard work and sober thinking.

"Two more," Gwen said impatiently. "What's in those?"

The two final packages contained a good-looking wool muffler from Midge and a book from Dr. Joe. Cherry felt a warm glow when she opened his present; it meant that he had completely forgiven her for that foolishness with Midge.

"Maybe you'll have another surprise," Bertha hinted, and got to her feet. There were sounds in Crowley corridor of nurses getting ready for supper. They all suddenly realized Christmas Eve was almost upon them, and rose to go.

"What do you mean, Bertha? Hey," Cherry recalled, "you did some hinting at supper a couple of times, too. What's up?"

But Bertha laughed and trooped out with the others.

Alone in her room, Cherry could not resist taking a peek at the cherished dress. She could barely wait for evening to come and put it on. Just then a rap came at her door.

"Ann?"

"No. It's me,"

Cherry didn't know who "me" was but she called, "Come on in!" and hastily put the dress away. No one came in. There was another timid rap. Cherry went to the door and yanked it open. There stood Mildred Burnham.

Cherry was amazed. It was the first time that the girl had made any move toward her. She must be in trouble, something must be wrong. Cherry remembered their last, unfortunate interview, and despite herself, she stiffened. She asked Mildred in.

"Thank you, but I won't come in. It's late and—uh—you have to get ready for the party, I guess." Mildred gulped. Her heavy sallow face was flushed.

"There's no hurry, and you know I'm always late anyhow," Cherry smiled. Joking concealed her mixed feelings. "I'm known around here as the late Miss Ames!" To her amazement, Mildred Burnham smiled back. Well, this was news! Perhaps this was what Bertha had been hinting about. But what did Mildred want of her?

The girl in the gray uniform shifted from one foot to the other. "I found out something," she mumbled. "I mean, I learned today is your birthday and—well, here!" She thrust a flat white box at Cherry.

It was Cherry's turn to gulp. "You—you brought me a present?" Mildred had turned a dull red. It was not easy for her to make any display of emotion, even this conventional one. Cherry herself was so surprised and puzzled she groped for words.

"What did I do to deserve this? I ought to be opening it, instead of standing here wondering what's in it!" She seized Mildred's hand and drew her into the room. Mildred sat down unhappily on the edge of a chair. Cherry, as she untied the ribbon, asked herself, "Yes, honestly, what did I do to deserve this? I scolded her, I was disgusted with her, I've completely ignored her recently . . . and she turns around and gives me a present!"

When she opened the box, she found a half dozen hand-drawn, hand-hemmed handkerchiefs. Mildred obviously had made them, and they must have taken a great deal of patient work. But why? Why? It could only mean that Mildred wanted to be friends after all. As Cherry admired and thanked Mildred for the handkerchiefs, she was trying to figure out the reason for this sudden change. And she was suffused with a burning sense of shame at her own prejudice and intolerance. Why, the very first time she had laid eyes on Mildred Burnham, she had taken a dislike to her!

"No one ever bothered to make things by hand for me before." Cherry gratefully smiled at her.

Mildred was edging out into the hall. "I'm glad you like them." Her rather lumpy figure slumped, then straightened. "Good-by."

"Good-by and thanks an awful lot and be sure you come again!"

Cherry watched her go, then closed the door, wondering. She was glad that she could report to Miss Reamer, now, that their relations had improved. Mildred's sudden change of behavior was a mystery indeed. Cherry would have to solve it later, because now she had to dash for supper, then hurry back and dress for the doctors' party. Church bells were ringing in the distance, happy laughter resounded in the corridor, out in the yard in the deep blue dusk an immense fir tree glistened with snow and ropes of blue lights. It was already Christmas Eve.

CHAPTER VIII

Black Lace

NINE O'CLOCK! CHERRY HAD THE DREAM DRESS ON. LEX'S flowers had arrived. She peered at herself in the small mirror and sighed with satisfaction. Diaphanous black chiffon clung and swirled about her, airy as smoke. Narrow black lace fluttered at the edge of the pert short skirt, delicate shadowy lace lay softly across Cherry's shoulders and the hollow of her throat. Lex's cool white gardenias were pinned in her jet-black hair, and she wore a single small strand of pearls. She certainly did not feel like her work-a-day self! Anything could happen tonight—romance, adventure, *anything!* She splurged with Charlie's perfume, snatched up her heavy coat, and ran into the hall.

"Cherry! Let's see you!" Gwen shrieked. A bevy of girls were chattering and pirouetting for one another in the corridor. "Look at siren Ames, will you? And just *smell* her! Gosh, Cherry!" they all exclaimed at once. "And, Ann! Why, no one'd ever know it was *us!*"

Every girl had contrived to appear her loveliest. Ann was in blue, a rich soft simple dress that made her blue eyes glow, and she wore the heavy twisted gold jewelry that had belonged to her grandmother.

"You look like something out of a portrait!" Cherry declared.

Gwen whirled around in her crackling cinnamon-colored taffeta, which made her red hair seem on fire. Bertha and Vivian had proudly made their own dresses: Vivian's was a flaring black skirt and a foamy white chiffon blouse; Bertha's Dresden-like flower print set off her fresh pastel coloring and candid eyes. Josie blinked without her glasses, but she looked very appealing in a red-and-white candy stripe and a crisp red bow in her hair. Marie Swift wore urbane gray, and Mai Lee's dress was encrusted with Chinese embroideries. Cherry was the only one who had flowers. She was glad no one asked who had sent them. Lex was misunderstood enough as it was.

"Quite a fashion show!" Cherry applauded. "Now come on, or the doctors will send out a searching party!"

They dived into coats and overshoes and started out across the snowy yard, holding scarfs over their heads so that their hair would not blow. Cherry's excitement mounted at the orchestra's first strains of lilting music, Behind her, Josie was crying, "Operating Room! Heaven help me, we start next week!"

Lex met her at the door.

"Like them?" he asked.

Cherry bent her head. "Just sniff," she laughed. "They're sumptuous! Thank you, Lex."

"Let's see you."

"Can't you wait till I get my coat off? Do you expect me to dance in these overshoes?" Cherry teased. "Are we going to fight right off or would you prefer to fight later in the evening?"

"Stand still!" he commanded. He looked at her critically and Cherry stood up very straight. A smile slowly spread over his intent face. "Very nice. Very nice indeed. You look like an advertisement for how to be beautiful."

"You look pretty nice yourself," Cherry replied. The sharp black and white of Lex's dinner clothes emphasized his decided black brows, his surprisingly light tawny hair. He wore his dinner clothes easily; they made him look older and more important than she had realized. "I'd better call you Dr. Upham," she decided. "Or 'sir'."

"Don't try it. Go get that coat off."

"Yes, Dr. Upham. Yes, sir," and Cherry vanished hastily into the ladies' cloakroom.

Out in the big Spencer lounge, which the doctors and internes had made festive with boughs of fir and fresh holly, the party was just starting. The poignant notes of *Stardust* filled the room. Only two couples bravely rose and circled around the empty gleaming dance floor. Girls in their rainbow dresses stood chatting with men in sleek black and white, but no one could quite forget that it was Nurse This and Doctor That. No one wanted to be the first, either, to approach the tempting buffet table with its sparkling punch bowl. No one could get started. The orchestra swung through two more songs, but still the dance floor remained almost completely deserted. People stood around in frozen little groups.

"How awful," Cherry whispered to Lex. "What this crowd needs is a stick of dynamite."

"Hold on to your hat," he whispered back, and walked rapidly away from her. To Cherry's surprise, he mounted the orchestra leader's little platform and said something to the young man.

The music broke off short. Everyone turned around, surprised. Out of the sudden hush, Lex dug his hands in his pockets and called out authoritatively, "We're going to start off with a square dance. Ladies over here, gentlemen opposite. Miss Cherry Ames will lead the ladies, Dr. "Ding" Jackson will lead the gentlemen." As everyone looked unwilling to move, Lex prodded them, "Come one, come all, all ready for the big square dance!

Here we go!" Two straggly lines formed, and a few started to dance. Then as the tune grew livelier and Lex called out sing-song, "Docey-do to the *right!* Swing your partner right *about—*" everyone, the whole room, was dancing. Up and down the long lines they skipped, bowing, clapping, circling, flushed with laughter. By the time the music stopped, everyone had entered into the spirit of the evening.

The self-consciousness had vanished, the party had begun. Before they could catch their breaths, Lex called out, "Conga line next! Miss Gwen Jones will lead!" He was smiling broadly, having a wonderful time. The drums and maracas began to beat out a fast insistent rhythm. "One-two-three-*kick!*" they sped hilariously in a huge snake-line around the room, dipping and turning as fast as they could, following Gwen's red head and the high-spirited song. A few fell out of line, breathless, but the rest of them conga'ed till the final merry tom-tom.

"Mercy!" someone cried out to Lex. "Have pity!"

"Not a chance, you sissies!" Lex shouted back, then quickly turned again to the orchestra leader. In a moment the band was playing the *St. Louis Blues.* Nobody's feet could say no to this popular number. The floor was crowded with dancers. A few drifted to the punch bowl. A few frankly sat down in laughing groups. The party was going. The party was a success. Lex ran down on the dance floor, cut in on "Ding," and danced Cherry away.

"Good work!" she beamed at him.

Apparently everyone else thought so, too. For the first time people were patting the learned and stormy Dr. Upham on the shoulder, calling him by his first name, joking with him. He joked back across the music, with his arm tight about Cherry's waist, and she saw his obvious pleasure.

"It's a good party," he confided to her happily. Cherry knew what he meant.

"It's a *very* good party," Cherry replied, delighted.

At eleven-thirty—the doctors' Christmas entertainment was scheduled for the stroke of midnight—Miss Reamer arrived. The Superintendent of Nurses was stately in a long violet dress. Usually, at their parties, she circulated for a little while among the guests. This evening, however, Miss Reamer went directly to the platform and held up her hand for silence.

"I'm sorry to break in on your party with this announcement," she said. "It looks like a very nice party. But unfortunately someone will have to miss the entertainment. An extra doctor and nurse are needed immediately. We're shorthanded—again—as usual." Miss Reamer looked around the room. "Would anyone care to volunteer?"

Lex, at Cherry's side, whispered instantly, "Come on, Cherry, it's a chance to be together." He raised his hand.

She hesitated. Lex pinched her arm hard. Cherry raised her hand, too.

"Thanks very much," Miss Reamer said. "Miss Ames, will you go right up to Men's Surgical? Dr. Upham, you're needed on your own ward."

Lex looked so crestfallen, so dumbfounded, that Cherry doubled up with laughter. "Lex—Lex—" she gasped. "Don't look like that—think of your duty——"

"I'm thinking of you," Lex grumbled and stamped off like a disappointed small boy without another word.

Cherry ran back through the snow from Spencer to Crowley, changed quickly into uniform, and hurried back to Spencer where the ward was. She went upstairs, thinking of the odd sensation she had experienced when she slipped off her black lace dress and donned the uniform. It was as if she were giving up all the happiness and reward that the black lace dress stood for—no, not exactly. It was merely that the hospital uniform came first. The black lace dress was still there, and she was earning the right to enjoy it with a free mind.

"Puritan!" Cherry laughed at herself, as she entered the darkened ward. "Why, you early American!" But her sense of duty was deep and strong. She would not have had it otherwise—and absolutely not in wartime, when her country, and therefore her own fate, was in danger.

Cherry worked hard for an hour at the doctor's direction. It was Dr. Randall, a surgeon whom she knew only by sight. The patient had suffered a hemorrhage, and Cherry assisted him in staunching the bleeding, cleansing the wound and putting on a fresh dressing. Meanwhile, the night nurse from an adjoining ward temporarily patrolled this ward as well as her own. Cherry's patient, an elderly man, was in a serious condition.

"Look at him every half-hour. Call me if there's any bleeding," Dr. Randall ordered. "All right, thanks," he said to the night nurse, "you may go back to your own ward now. The night supervisor said Miss Ames will stay here all night. Thank you, Miss Ames." He turned, remembering. "And Merry Christmas!"

"Merry Christmas!" Cherry responded.

She was left alone on the sleeping ward.

"So this is a nurse's Christmas," Cherry thought. She began to pity herself a little. Cherry glanced down at her oxfords—just a while ago she had been wearing frivolous slippers. Those satin slippers had seemed so exciting, so important, early in the evening. Then she recalled the emergency preparations deep in the hospital basement, and the helpless premature babies curled up in their incubators. Now as she softly walked about the sleeping ward with her flashlight, the frivolous slippers were completely forgotten. Cherry heard a scratching and suppressed laughter at the ward door. She looked up.

Out in the lighted corridor, looking like huge butterflies in their soft-colored dresses, Ann and Gwen and Bertha and Josie and all her other friends were beckoning to her. Cherry slipped out to them.

"We came to tell you what you missed, you poor thing!" Ann whispered excitedly. "The entertainment——"

"——was the funniest thing I've ever seen!" Gwen interrupted. "They did a take-off on the head resident surgeon, and another of Miss Reamer, and then they had a zany play——"

The girls chattered on. Cherry listened to the details. They were loyal and dear to come, but to her surprise she was not much interested. Finally the girls slipped out, leaving a trail of laughter and scent.

"Good night and Merry Christmas," Cherry called after them.

She returned to the ward and went immediately to look at the hemorrhage patient. He was all right. "Now why wasn't I disappointed that I missed the entertainment?" Cherry wondered. The flashlight's beam brushed her starched white apron. Then Cherry understood. The white apron symbolized what Christmas stood for.

Cherry settled down at the head nurse's desk for the long, lonely night. The night before Christmas. The night of unselfish love and goodness and devotion.

Cherry glanced around the darkened, quiet ward. She gazed at the still figures in the beds, who were dependent upon her this night for their very lives. As she wrote out the night report, and got out gauze to roll into bandages, during the long still hours ahead, Cherry thought:

"This is the first Christmas in my life, I think, that I've realized to the full the spirit of Christmas."

~~~~~~

CHAPTER IX

Operating Room

THE NEW YEAR STARTED OFF WITH A BANG. CHERRY'S doughty old enemy and friend, Dr. Wylie, unexpectedly came back to the hospital on a short leave from the Army Medical Corps. Cherry, recalling her past conflicts with the grumpy surgeon, felt that it might be only a matter of time before she would tangle with him again.

Operating Room loomed just ahead! Cherry was assigned to Women's Surgical Ward and sometime during this three-month period, she would be called for O.R. That was the acid test . . . and Cherry looked forward to it with much trepidation and misgiving. As a further maddening touch, those of Cherry's classmates who were already operating seniors dashed in and out of her room, shouting and moaning such verdicts as, "It's awful—I'm petrified—I'll be the death of somebody yet!"

. . . "Most wonderful thing! But hard!" . . . "Cherry, wait till you're called! I'm warning you! Just wait!"

"Just keep calm," she advised herself frantically, as she sat in the lecture hall. The class was having a review of aseptic procedure, preparatory to going on Operating Room. Cherry had learned in her first year how to keep articles free from germs, or sterile, and in her junior year how to care for patients before and after surgery, but those courses had been easy and elementary compared to this senior work. They were having a great many lectures, a great deal of preparation for O.R.

Meanwhile, working on Women's Surgical as a senior was very different, too, from the work she had done on Women's Surgical Ward as a first-year student. Then she had given bed baths and simple care to post-operative patients who were nearly well. But the patients Cherry now cared for only recently had come down from Operating Room. They were helpless and seriously ill, and required the closest charting, difficult techniques, and expert care. As a senior, Cherry had the heavier responsibilities of giving medications, treatments, and also charting for the whole ward. But Cherry was relieved to leave bedmaking and baths to the first-year nurses and do the more complicated work herself.

There was one patient on the ward who watched Cherry sympathetically as she worked in the long, quiet, white room lined with high, narrow, white beds. This patient happened to be the only woman on the ward who was already convalescing and was ambulatory. She was allowed by the doctor to be up and about for a few hours a day. She was a plump cheerful woman of sixty, who had been a practical nurse. Everyone called her "Mom." She was quite alone in the world, and poor.

Mom had been a farm girl in Minnesota. When she was fifteen, the farm had burned down and only she had survived. Kindly nuns took her in and from them she learned practical nursing. Alone, and stunned by what had happened to her, Mom dedicated her life to serving others. All this Mom had gradually confided to Cherry.

One bitter day, snow and sleet raged out of an overcast sky. The electric lights had been on all day. Even the bustling, self-contained, clean white world of the hospital seemed gloomy in these long winter months. Cherry went about her work on the ward, wishing that Operating Room would hurry up and assign her. She started to turn a helpless patient in bed, when Mom called out:

"Don't lift her that way, honey! You'll strain your back! You dassn't lift without a helper."

Cherry looked up, surprised. She smiled at the elderly woman who was earnestly shaking her gray head at her. "You're right, Mom, but there's no one around to assist." She again arranged the two propping pillows at the side of the bed and murmured encouragement to the sick woman.

"And what's the matter with me to assist!" Cherry had slipped her hands under the patient's shoulders and hips, when she glanced up again. Mom was walking toward her, unsteady but determined. Cherry was horrified and exclaimed:

"Get back in bed! You've been up long enough!"

"Won't!" Mom struggled with her vivid kimono, hung on to a chair, and reached Cherry's side. "I'm a sort of nurse myself, anyhow."

"You're too weak to lift!" Cherry cried. "Get back in bed! You know the nurse is boss!"

"Don't sass your elders," Mom said as she, too, slipped her hands under the helpless woman. "Over she goes!" and automatically Cherry slid the woman to the propped pillows, flexed her knees, then drew the woman onto her side. Mom competently stuffed pillows behind the patient's back and between her knees. "That's to support her," Mom announced, out of breath but proud. "You obeyed me like a real good girl."

"Well, I didn't mean to!" Cherry retorted, amused and flustered. "And now, please, please, get back into bed."

"No, ma'am," Mom said happily. "It feels good to be up and useful. I'll tell you what. From now on, I'm your assistant."

Cherry bit her lip to keep from laughing. "Mom, you're incorrigible. Must I call the doctor to get him to *order* you back into bed?"

"Call him, but it won't do any good," Mom said, unrepentant. And she wandered around the ward, folding towels and straightening blankets and thoroughly enjoying herself. When Cherry saw how it satisfied the old lady to be busy, she asked the head nurse about it. The head nurse approved letting Mom stay up, and promised to get the doctor's order on it as soon as possible. After all, to convalesce Mom had to get her mind off her illness and take an interest in outside things.

Mom proved to be more of an "assistant" than Cherry had bargained for. In the next few days, Cherry found, on the lower shelves of the linen closet where Mom could reach them, towels folded incorrectly, instruments out of place in the utility room, and Miss Waters's flowers on Mrs. King's bedside table.

"But Miss Waters has so many flowers and she's too sick even to see them and that poor Mrs. King didn't have a single blossom!" Mom explained. "So I just evened things up a little."

Cherry did not have the heart to scold Mom. "What about the linens? And the instruments?" she asked sternly.

Mom looked apologetic, and fingered her two short curly gray braids. "I expect I'm not a real nurse like you.

I never had any good training like you and mostly my uniform was just a housedress." Her face crinkled up in a smile. "But I nursed a lot of people and brought a lot of babies into this old world and—" Her smile faded. "I tried to do the right things, but maybe I did 'em the wrong way."

"I'll bet you've done a lot of good," Cherry consoled her.

One evening, when Cherry was on duty from three to eleven, Mom insisted upon helping her serve the supper trays. She beamed so, padding from bed to bed, that Cherry could practically see Mom's chart showing her physical improvement. Besides, Cherry was growing fond of the game old lady in her violently colored and checkered kimono. Her unquenchable good spirits helped against the difficult work on the ward and the black howling night outside.

"I'll just take a look to see that everything's going all right in the kitchen," Mom said importantly as she ambled out of the ward.

Suddenly the lights went out. The ward, in the midst of supper, was plunged into darkness. Cherry groped her way into the darkened corridor. Shouts and questions and faint expletives came from the other wards. The whole floor was left in blackness. Flashlights went on quickly. Out of the clamor, Cherry heard a quavering voice call her name.

"Yes?" Cherry followed the sound down the inky corridor. "Who's calling Cherry Ames?"

Then she heard loud weeping. She half-fell into a closet and there was Mom, one bare foot entangled with an electric cord.

"I stumbled. These old slippers never did fit me! Oh me, oh my, what an awful thing I've gone and done! Got all tangled up in this—this—" Mom blew her nose hard.

"Never mind." Cherry knelt and focused her flashlight. Because of repairs in progress, one plug temporarily controlled the whole floor. She plugged in the connection, and all the lights went on again. "Never mind, Mom."

"What are they going to do to me?" Mom pleaded. "If they put me out, I haven't got a place or a soul to turn to."

Cherry soothed her and promised her she would not be turned out of the hospital until she was much better. She got Mom back into bed. The old lady was exhausted from her adventure.

Later that evening, when the rest of the ward was asleep, they had a little talk.

"I'm not just an old fool," Mom said soberly. "But I'm an old work-horse that's used to the harness, and I can't abide lying here idle, specially when I see you with your hands full. But if I hinder you more than I help you, you just speak up."

"I know how you feel," Cherry said. "And now that you're getting well, you need a little change. If one of the nurse's aides on day duty has time, she might take you for a tour in a wheel chair, or up to the sun roof."

Cherry tried to make it sound tempting, but Mom shook her head.

"You don't have to coddle me. I've seen too much real trouble in my time to need a stick of sugar candy. I'll get well and on my own two feet because," Mom said slowly, "maybe I'll be seeing some real trouble again right soon."

Cherry wondered what was worrying the old lady. She wondered, too, if Mom wanted to talk and get it off her mind, as patients sometimes did with their nurses. But Mom closed her mouth in a tight, determined line. Cherry, of course, did not pry.

That was the last Cherry saw of Mom for the next week, except for a few occasional minutes. One morning she saw the notice on the bulletin board: Ames, C., to O.R. Here it was! Cherry sent word to Mom via one of the ward juniors—she could just imagine Mom's hearty "Good luck!" ringing in her ears—and ran off. It seemed to her that the elevator had never ascended so slowly.

For all her eagerness to go on Operating Room, Cherry felt a little panic too. She remembered sensational things she had read in the newspapers or had seen in the movies—fearful things, secret masked figures in white with sharp eyes, hints of morbid drugs and cruel instruments and lurking death. Could Operating Room really be like that? And her classmates had brought back such weird, conflicting reports. The elevator door opened. Cherry stepped out. Her hands were cold with nervousness.

Cherry got over her nervousness in the first five minutes. This was no dire half-world—this was the sane, efficient hospital going about its miraculous business. Surgery was simply a more miraculous branch of medicine, its daring equaled by its skill and by its strict techniques. Cherry, of course, had seen O.R.'s before, but now they were her personal business!

The white-tiled Operating Rooms were furnished with a high long table under a powerful center lamp and smaller wheeled tables for adrenalin, hypodermics, morphine, and for sterile trays of instruments, solutions, and gauze. Down the hall there was the Instrument Room, the walls of which were lined with instruments. Daylight flooded in through enormous windows. Just off the Operating Rooms were one or more small tiled rooms with sinks for scrubbing up. The air was sweet and warm, and smelled faintly of ether and soap and water. Also on this floor was the blood bank. Cherry found it all highly reassuring and fascinating.

"May I assist on an operation today?" she eagerly asked the regular operating nurse.

The graduate nurse smiled at her ruefully and handed her a list. "You may read this list of the day's scheduled operations. Come into my office and I'll explain about making supplies. Then I'll show you what the various surgical instruments look like and tell you how they're used and how you are to sterilize them. Then you may," she cocked an amused eye at her bewildered student nurse and grinned, "set up a nurse's table for a tonsillectomy." It was an anticlimax.

"But not assist at an operation?"

The operating nurse shook her head. "For the first few days, you'll just set up tables, and make supplies and drains to use in O.R., and generally keep your eyes open. You'll be a 'dirty nurse'—not sterile—you'll be a messenger who goes in and out of O.R. without contaminating anything. Later on, I'll teach you how to put on a sterile gown and set up a sterile table and help drape a patient and handle general supplies. And *then*, at long last, the supervisor will assign you to jobs helping the surgeons." Cherry looked woebegone. "But right now you can watch an operation."

"Watch what?" Cherry breathed.

The nurse laughed outright. "In there." She pointed to a swinging door with a high glass window. "The surgeon will lecture as he operates."

Cherry found that this Operating Room had seats built up around it, like a miniature balcony at the theater. Some of her classmates were already there, waiting. Whispered information was passed from one nervous student to another: "It's going to be a simple appendix." "Who's the surgeon?" "Don't know but I heard it's someone important." "I wonder if I can stand the sight of blood." "Oh, there's Ames! How's your friend Dr. Upham, Cherry?" "Hush! They're wheeling in the patient."

Everyone fell silent as two orderlies gently rolled in a table bearing the unconscious patient. The man had not come from the ether room, so Cherry knew he must have had that wonderful Avertin, an anaesthetic administered rectally. The two orderlies placed the patient on the operating table. He was dressed in the short hospital gown and operating room boots. An operating nurse came in, in sterile gown, mask, gloves, and cap which completely covered her hair. She did not touch the patient. A non-sterile nurse—the "dirty nurse"—checked the patient's pulse and respiration and seemed satisfied. A sterile nurse was preparing trays, lifting sterile things which the surgeon would need onto a sterile tray with sterile forceps. Cherry was sharply aware of how the element of infection, or hemorrhage, or shock, or any other risk, was held rigidly in control.

Then the interne entered, held the door open respectfully, and the surgeon came in. Cherry blinked and looked again. The surgeon was Dr. Wylie! He was wearing cap and mask. He glared at the class and at the assisting nurses, a formidable stocky little figure with icy gray eyes showing over the mask. A nurse helped him into his sterile coat, then slipped sterile rubber gloves over his steely fingers.

Cherry speculated fleetingly as to why a world-famous surgeon with a limited leave should bother to do this simple operation and give this lecture. Perhaps it was a whim. Dr. Wylie had a lot of stubborn whims and fixed ideas, Cherry recalled with a grin and a slight shudder.

They started. A cradle of sterile sheets was set up around the patient. The operating nurse exposed a small abdominal area, and swabbed it. The second nurse kept constant check on the patient's condition. Dr. Wylie explained each step. Then the interne made the incision. Cherry had thought she would jump when that happened, but the incision was quick, sure, clean, Clamps were applied to the sides of the cavity so the surgeon could work freely.

Dr. Wylie started to work, lecturing to the class at the same time. Cherry followed it well. What amazed her was the way Dr. Wylie would stick his hand out, without a word, without turning away from the patient, and the operating nurse would put in his hand the right instrument or a swab or solution. How did she know and anticipate just what the surgeon needed at every minute or two of the quick, deft, ever-changing job? "That's what I'm up here to learn to do," Cherry realized, and hoped devoutly for powers of intuition.

From her high seat behind glass, Cherry could see the surgeon's hands moving among the complex living parts. Now they moved lightly and delicately; now they applied an instrument, carefully, quickly; now they tugged with real power. Dr. Wylie's voice grew a little breathless as he lectured. Occasionally he muttered an order and the nurse stepped up to wipe, to apply solution, and once to give adrenalin.

Then the real work was over, the incision was closed, and the wound was dressed. Orderlies lifted the patient from the operating table to a wheeled table and, accompanied by another nurse, carried the man back to the ward. Dr. Wylie stripped off his mask and rubber gloves.

"Questions?" he barked.

The class sat paralyzed under his fearsome glance. No one spoke.

"Hah! No questions," he said scornfully. He turned on his heel and strode out, his long white coat flapping harshly, as Cherry remembered so well.

After he had left, the class relaxed a little. The interne was still there. "Any questions?" he asked, and pretended to glare at them. The class laughed uproariously, and this time they had questions, lots of them.

When Cherry went back to the ward that afternoon, Mom called her over eagerly.

"How'd your first day go?" she asked.

Cherry felt a rush of gratitude as she stood beside the bed. Mom was really interested, really understanding. "It was pretty exciting. But I don't really have a job yet, not until next week when I go in on an operation."

"Next week! My, I'd like to be in your boots then!" She took Cherry's hand in hers. "Operating nurse, no less! But mind you don't wear yourself out with the excitement."

"Oh, I'm fine," Cherry laughed back, "and how are you?" She routinely picked up Mom's chart from beside her bed, and scowled at what she read. "Why, Mom, what kind of behavior is this?"

"I feel fine," Mom insisted staunchly.

"Not according to the chart," and Cherry put it back. She felt the concern she would feel for any patient, and something extra for Mom besides.

As for Dr. Wylie, Cherry met him, wearing his khaki uniform, several afternoons later in Dr. Fortune's laboratory. Lex was there, too, quite subdued in the presence of the famous surgeon. Cherry had told Lex of her scrapes and adventure with Dr. Wylie in her first year at Spencer, so he winked at her expectantly when Dr. Joe said:

"You remember Cherry Ames, don't you?"

"Certainly." Dr. Wylie shook hands with her. "Noticed her in Operating Room the other day. How are you, Miss

Ames? Still using that rouge, I see. Don't expect me to show you any favors on Operating." But his sharp features cracked in a cordial smile.

"I was about to explain to Dr. Wylie and Dr. Upham," Dr. Joe said, with his gray hair standing on end, "about an important discovery I made. Sit down, my dear, and listen too."

Cherry wanted to tell Dr. Joe that his thinking she could understand anything Dr. Wylie or Lex understood both complimented and frightened her. But she sat down obediently enough beside Lex and listened.

"You know, Cherry, that illness is caused by infection, by germs or bacteria entering and lodging in the body—unwanted and dangerous lodgers, I might say," Dr. Joe started. "Our problem is how to kill the germs."

"Remember the magic bullet?" Lex spoke up. "The great researcher, Paul Ehrlich, wanted to find something you could just shoot at the bacteria."

"But he never found it," Dr. Wylie said dryly. "And no one else has been able to find it."

"Aren't," Cherry said uncertainly, "aren't those new sulfa drugs powerful germ-killers?"

"Good girl," Dr. Joe said approvingly. "Sulfa seems nearly like a miracle. But penicillin——"

"But penicillin!" Lex interrupted excitedly. "It's even better. Why it can——"

"Penicillin!" Dr. Wylie exclaimed and leaped to his feet. "It saves lives that sulfa can't save! It goes on when sulfa breaks down!"

"Penicillin!" Cherry joined in the general excitement. That was the wonderful drug everybody was talking about! She remembered reading about it. "I know!" Cherry's eyes danced with excitement. "That's the drug that was found by British researchers . . . and only very little of it can be made at a time . . . and the government controls the distribution because every speck of it must go to our boys in the armed forces . . . and it must be kept a secret from the enemy . . . and only a few researchers in America are allowed to have it for research work . . . and they're working hard to find a method to produce it in large quantities and . . . and . . ." Cherry stopped breathlessly. She puzzled a moment, then asked, "But what *exactly* is penicillin?"

"Bravo, Cherry!" cried Lex. "What *exactly* is penicillin? It's a mold that puts a chemical vacuum around the germs and cuts them off from their oxygen supply so that they can't breathe. Hence our little enemies die of asphyxiation."

"That's Penicillin A which Dr. Upharn just described," Dr. Wylie further explained. "Only recently, Penicillin B was found at the St. Louis University. Penicillin B, Miss Ames, surrounds the bacteria with too much oxygen, instead of too little like A, and literally burns the germs alive."

"And when we learn how to handle A and B together," Dr. Joe declared, "it will be one of the greatest victories in man's fight against disease." Dr. Joe's tired eyes shone as he stood there, clutching a laboratory report in one hand and a test tube in the other. All eyes were glued on him. "And, gentlemen—" he paused and there was a moment's expectant silence— "I have found a way to synthesize new members of this acridine group, more potent than either A or B, into a *new* penicillin-like chemical, so that it can be produced commercially by a pharmaceutical house— not just in the laboratory."

Cherry was not quite sure that she understood, but she did know that big things for the future of medicine were going on in Dr. Joe's laboratory, *at this very moment*. She shook her head dazedly.

"That means, Cherry," Dr. Joe continued, "that we can take it out of the laboratory and make it commercially in large quantities and fairly cheaply. In time this wonder-chemical will be available to everybody."

A stunned silence followed his announcement. Lex let out a low whistle and Dr. Wylie said slowly, "But no one as yet has been able to achieve that synthesis. Are you sure, Fortune?"

"Yes, I am sure. It can be done."

Dr. Wylie jumped up and began nervously pacing back and forth. The others watched him silently. Suddenly he wheeled and faced them. "Do you realize what this means? Do you realize that we have a most important military secret on our hands—one that must be guarded with our lives? . . . Fortune, we must report your findings to the government authorities at once!"

"Not yet, Dr. Wylie, not yet!" Dr. Joe shook his head. "I have some further research work to do on my formula, before it can be turned over to the proper authorities."

"Whe-e-ew!" Lex exclaimed. "Wouldn't the enemy love to get his hands on a thing like this!"

"Exactly!" Dr. Wylie agreed. "And that's not the only thing," he said, and he looked worried. "There's another great danger! . . . Thieves! . . . Plain crooks! . . . There's great wealth in it for whatever pharmaceutical house can manufacture it first—or get sole rights. And there's big money in it for whoever sells the formula. Such things have been stolen before." He suddenly glanced at the doors and windows. "You'd better put your stuff in a safer place than this building."

There was a heavy silence. Dr. Wylie cleared his throat and went on reluctantly. "You're such a careless and absent-minded sort, Fortune, if you don't mind my saying so." He frowned at Dr. Joe affectionately. "I'd like to ask you several questions. Who else knows about this? Who has keys to Lincoln Hall? Who has keys to this laboratory?"

Only the four present knew about it. A few staff doctors and researchers, the building superintendent and two watchmen, whose reputations all were above reproach, had keys to Lincoln. Only Dr. Joe and Lex had keys to this laboratory.

Dr. Wylie looked at Lex critically. "I don't believe I've met Dr. Upham before this afternoon."

Lex twisted uncomfortably in his chair. Cherry was shocked at Dr. Wylie's attitude toward Lex. "But surely," she thought, "Dr. Wylie has no suspicions." It was only that he himself was so meticulous, and he knew other people were less careful. And he was, Cherry realized, deeply concerned for the safety of this drug.

Dr. Joe explained how Lex happened to be assisting him at his research.

Dr. Wylie said, "So you sought Dr. Fortune out and solicited this job. Why?"

Lex turned red. Cherry wished he realized that Dr. Wylie meant no offense. Lex looked Dr. Wylie firmly in the eye. "Miss Ames is frequently here, and I wanted to see her."

"Humph! You don't look like a romantic sort," Dr. Wylie thought aloud. "Upham, before you asked to work with Dr. Fortune, did you know what sort of research he was engaged in?"

Dr. Joe said eagerly, "He knew very specifically. Why, he studied up intensively, so I couldn't refuse to take him on!" Dr. Joe's tone was amused and grateful. But the facts evidently made an entirely different impression on Dr. Wylie.

Lex stood up. He was angry. "I don't like the implications of your remarks, Dr. Wylie," he said point-blank. "I'll give up my key and stop coming here, at once, if Dr. Fortune wishes it."

"No, no, nothing of the sort," Dr. Joe said gently. "Sit down, son. You've been a great help to me and I need you too much to let you go."

Both Dr. Wylie and Lex were silenced. Lex sat down again. Then he got up restlessly and busied himself at the long laboratory table. Cherry went over to him and they talked in low voices.

"Are you coming to the Lincoln's Birthday dance?" she asked him.

"I haven't the time."

She said uncertainly, "I didn't know you're so busy."

He evaded her eyes. His whole figure, his clenched hands, were tense. "I'm doing some extra work," he said.

"Heavens, Lex, you're already working too hard as it is. You'll kill yourself off, working."

He shifted from one foot to the other as if annoyed. Finally he said, "I've got to make some money."

"Why, what do you want with money?" Cherry teased him.

He looked embarrassed. "You'd be surprised, Cherry. You really would."

Well, Lex certainly was behaving strangely, Cherry thought. She decided it was because he was still smarting from Dr. Wylie's questions. Lex's pride was his sore point, anyway.

As they were leaving, Dr. Wylie said warningly, "No one is to talk about this. There must be no knowledge of this secret spread around the hospital!"

They all agreed. Yet Cherry was to hear talk about it within the hour. And, curiously enough, it was to come from Mom.

~~~~~~

CHAPTER X

Mom Talks

A STRANGE PURPLISH LIGHT FILLED THE YARD WHEN Cherry left Dr. Joe's laboratory. The hospital buildings seemed insubstantial pieces of white paper. The wind had risen. It was going to snow and storm any minute. She had half an hour before she was due on the ward, and she was passing the residence hall for the first-year and junior students.

"It's a good chance to see Mildred Burnham," Cherry thought. "I haven't even been to see her since she brought me those handkerchiefs. It's not very nice of me."

But every time she had tried to be "nice" to Mildred, the girl had rebuffed her efforts. The only time Mildred Burnham had been friendly with Cherry was after Cherry had let her severely alone. Perhaps that was the way to treat the perverse girl—backwards! It certainly seemed to Cherry that Mildred reacted in reverse. Just then the storm broke, and Cherry ducked into the residence hall.

Mildred was in, studying. She looked at Cherry expressionlessly, but she did say, "Come in."

Cherry went into Mildred's room and paused at the open textbook. "Hmm, hot wet dressings," she said. "I always had trouble with those. I still do."

Mildred looked mollified. "I have a knack with them. Please sit down, Cherry."

Cherry sat down, thinking, "So that's the tack! Treat her like an equal, not an adoptee." But there was a strained silence.

"How do you like the heavy ward work you're doing now?" Cherry asked.

"All right. I'm doing all right at it, too," Mildred added defensively.

There was another of those awful silences. Cherry tried to think of something that would bolster Mildred's shaky self-assurance, so that she would not have to remain on the defensive. Cherry opened her small purse and took out one of the handkerchiefs Mildred had made for her at Christmas.

"These are my pride and joy," Cherry said. She spread the handkerchief on the dark wood of the desk so that the drawnwork pattern showed. "Ever so many people have admired them and asked me where I got them."

Mildred's heavy face lost its sullenness. "I like making things, doing practical things. I guess that's why I like nursing."

"We've got that in common," Cherry smiled. There followed another dead pause. Finally Mildred said:

"Are you through on the ward for today or do you have to go on now?"

Cherry took the hint and rose. "You're right, I'm due there any minute. I'll leave you to your hot wet dressings."

Mildred closed the door on her. In fact, Mildred virtually put her out.

Cherry hurried over to Spencer Hall. She was so exasperated and discouraged that her interest in Mildred Burnham died. Until today, Cherry had charitably assumed that Mildred had some sort of quirk and found personal relations difficult. But it was plain now that Mildred simply did not like her. Well, that was Mildred's right. Any further attempts to be the interested and guiding senior would amount to forcing herself on Mildred. Cherry ran up the steps of Spencer and a definite decision formed in her mind.

This was the end. She would go to Miss Reamer, explain that she and Mildred could not get along—being very careful to shed no bad light on the younger girl—and ask to be released from the "adoption." It was too bad, but it probably was what Mildred herself wanted. Until she could find time to see Miss Reamer, she would let Mildred strictly alone. Cherry felt relieved.

It was consoling to be back, even temporarily, on the warm, quiet, well-lighted ward. It was especially consoling to talk to Mom. Cherry had grown attached to the warm-hearted old lady. Mom's condition, during the time Cherry was on O.R., had gradually become worse. She was more ill now than when Cherry had first met her. But Mom managed to sit up on her elbows and demand of Cherry:

"You look as solemn as an owl and as cross as a bear! Who bit you?"

Cherry laughed. "You already know who bit me." Cherry had told Mom about her troubles with Mildred, and now she related the latest fiasco.

"If you ask me," Mom said, "you could spare a bit more kindness to that girl. There's plenty of folks like her, but there's plenty of ways to get around 'em." She turned over with difficulty as Cherry started to apply a scultetus binder, to support Mom's wound.

"I don't like the looks of this," Cherry muttered. She picked up Mom's chart. "I don't like it at all." She would notify the head nurse of Mom's condition at once. The doctor would have to be consulted. It crossed her mind that Mom might have to have a second operation. It not infrequently happened that a stubborn condition required a series of operations, spaced far enough apart to let the patient regain strength for each surgery. Only yesterday the graduate nurse on this ward had said something about Mom's changed condition.

"What else'd you do this afternoon?" Mom asked, making faces as Cherry pressed down the tails of the binder.

"I went to Dr. Joe's lab. There was a big surgeon there—one who might have to operate on you if you don't make up your mind to get well."

"Was that nice young doctor there? What did you all talk about?"

"Lie down now. And stop making such awful faces. We talked about Dr. Joe's research."

"Mmm, must have been interesting. Say, could it've been about—I can't remember the word, can't remember anything any more—hand me that newspaper, honey—" Cherry found the folded newspaper. "Here it is." Mom's work-worn finger traveled down the news items. "Penicillin. Is that what your Dr. Joe's making?"

Cherry felt the blood leap to her cheeks. She whirled around. "What ever made you say that?" she demanded.

Mom looked at her in innocent amazement. "I don't know. I just thought that might be it." She tugged awkwardly at her curly gray braids. "Don't know why I thought so. Just thought so."

Cherry felt a sinking sensation in the pit of her stomach. She did not believe in such things as intuition or mental telepathy. And Mom did not think this for no reason at all. She must have heard something to make her think it. Everybody was Mom's friend, she must hear a lot. Cherry sat down on a chair beside Mom's bed and said to the old lady gently:

"Try to remember if you heard anyone say anything about penicillin or about Dr. Joe."

Mom furrowed her forehead and bit her lip and tugged hard at her braids. At last she said, "Seems to me—yes, that's right, all right. Day before yesterday, it was. The maid was telling me she heard that Dr. Joe was making this stuff with the funny name that the government's making such a to-do about."

Cherry tried to keep her voice steady. "Which maid was that?"

"The little one with the false teeth that don't fit her. But she gave up her place here yesterday. She told me about this when she came to say good-by to me. She knows I'm a sort of a nurse."

So the maid had left. Why? Where to? The maid here had been a trustworthy woman, so far as Cherry knew. Cherry tried to think.

"If the maid worked over here in Spencer, Mom, how did she know what was going on in another building?"

"She heard. You know how you hear things in a big place like this hospital. The cleaning woman in Lincoln Hall is an old friend of hers."

Cherry knew the cleaning woman, Alma Jarvis. Mrs. Jarvis had worked in the hospital for twenty years. She was a widow who had raised four children, single-handed, and she was the soul of discretion. It was not like her to talk. Dr. Joe must have labeled the test tubes with their golden fluids, and carelessly left them in full view! And Mrs. Jarvis probably had recognized the name of the drug that was so publicized, and in her excitement confided the secret to the maid. Cherry frowned. Dr. Joe should have been more careful.

Mom asked anxiously. "Did I say anything wrong? What're you looking so pale about?"

"Listen to me, Mom. What you heard is just gossip. But it could do a great deal of harm. Promise me you'll say nothing more on the subject to anyone."

How she wished the cleaning woman had not let this dangerous secret leak out! The whole hospital would be excited about it—would talk of it in public, where anyone could hear!

Mom pressed her finger against her lips, her old eyes dancing. "I just love secrets. Mum's the word."

"Mum certainly is the word," Cherry said seriously. "I know you can keep a secret. I've been watching you keep your own worry to yourself, whatever it is."

Mom's face changed expression, and she sighed. " 'Tisn't much of a secret. I just don't want to worry you, honey, or make you feel bad. You've got your work to worry about, and that's enough."

"Mom, if there's anything I can do for you," Cherry said earnestly, "I wish you'd tell me."

"I'm going to be perfectly all right, just fine," Mom said. Her voice shook a little. "Now you run along about your work, child. Shoo!"

Cherry certainly had plenty of work to do on Women's Surgical Ward in the late afternoon. Besides, she and the other nurses supervised nurse's aides who "specialed" unconscious patients just brought down from Operating Room. These aides sat beside the patients watching constantly for the pale face and cold perspiration and rapid weak pulse which meant shock—and danger. It could mean hemorrhage, too. Cherry learned to reassure a patient just coming out of anaesthetic, in a calm, low voice. Even the routine tasks on this ward were special. The operative bed required rubber sheets, three covered hot water bags, to fight shock or bleeding, but no pillow.

Mom still managed to be a lovable nuisance, although she was seriously ill. Once Cherry entered the ward and was horrified to find Mom had shakily struggled out of bed and was giving a drink of water, instead of cracked ice, to a patient just emerged from anaesthesia—a procedure that could have made the woman choke or swallow her tongue. "But she licked her lips, she was thirsty," Mom said. "I guess I'm forgetting what little nursing I used to know."

There were new lectures now, too, senior courses in medical and surgical emergencies. Most important of all, there was Operating Room.

Cherry first went in on minor operations. Mostly she watched the surgeon and the nurse, and handed the nurse a few things at her low-voiced requests. The balance of the time, Cherry learned to keep the Operating Rooms ready for instant use—no small job, and Cherry became well acquainted with the autoclave, which sterilized dry things like bandages under steam pressure, with sterile solutions and with setting up tables of nurses' supplies correctly. A week of this training left Cherry with the fairly correct impression that being an operating nurse was quick, painstaking, tense work, but simple work. In the following weeks, when Cherry acted as first assistant on more complex operations, she felt almost nonchalant.

Cherry enjoyed most the drama and the personalities up here. Men and women said strange things to Cherry in the two or three minutes when they lay on the operating table, waiting for the surgeon to come in. Each surgeon and interne, too, entered the Operating Room with varied attitudes. Elderly Dr. Witherspoon, who was usually a gentle person, invariably stormed into the O.R. in a fury and raged until the operation was safely completed. Dr. Mary Vinson, on the other hand, was the coolest surgeon Cherry had yet seen. This woman was one of the very few to break into surgery, traditionally a man's field. She was wonderfully, undeviatingly good, moving with calm sure hands and steady eyes, without a trace of temperament or tension. But the first time Cherry laid eyes on Dr. Jenks, she whispered to the regular operating nurse:

"Look! It's a pixie!"

"I think he looks more like a gnome," the nurse whispered back.

He was a tiny little man with a funny cheerful face. His operating coat hung on him comically and his eyeglasses, almost bigger than he was, wobbled as he darted around the table.

"Good morning," he greeted the operating nurse. "And who's this? A new student nurse? Well, well, that's fine. We have a fine diseased kidney this morning, Miss— what's your name?—Ames. I hope you like kidney cases."

Cherry assured him respectfully that she did. They prepared the sleeping patient and began the precise mechanics of the operation. Little Dr. Jenks took an instrument in one hand and started to sing.

"Oh, *connais-tu un pays*," he sang, off key, while he bobbed about the horizontal patient on tiptoe. "Oh, *connais—con—con—*," he sang under his breath as the work grew harder. Cherry had to struggle with herself to keep from laughing. Suddenly the pixie's voice rose triumphantly. "Yes, *je connais un pays!*" The stubborn organ had yielded under his instrument. "Do you like music, Miss Ames?" he inquired happily.

"Yes, doctor," Cherry murmured. She moved quickly forward to put the small spade-shaped instrument in his hand. He did not hear her reply. He was scowling over the patient and grunting, "*Connais-tu. Connais-tu. Con—nais—tu——!*"

His hands were moving rapidly. Cherry and the nurse alertly watched, and helped. Once Dr. Jenks looked up and said, "You're a good operating nurse, Miss Ames. Very good. Very nice work."

"Thank you, doctor," Cherry murmured. Then he was singing again, at the top of his lungs, excruciatingly flat.

"He never sings anything else," the operating nurse laughed to Cherry after the surgeon had gone, "and he never gets to the end of that song. He's one of the best men in this part of the country. You ought to be proud he complimented you."

Cherry was proud. She still had occasional doubts about her nursing ability. Praise from a man like Dr. Jenks reassured her. Later that afternoon, leaving Spencer Hall for the special reference library in another building, Cherry did a little day-dreaming about the graduate's broad black velvet ribbon she would wear on her cap. Her half-decision, made that day in the Nursery, to nurse right here on the home front, came back to her. Nothing had happened to make her change her mind. She was wondering about her future when Lex's voice called her.

He was carrying a package. They went out of Spencer Hall together into the frozen yard. In spite of the still bitter cold of late winter, they walked slowly, looking into each other's faces.

"What's that?" Cherry asked, nodding toward the package.

"That's *it!*" Lex looked glum. "Dr. Joe is so lax, he puts off moving this stuff to a safer place. I took it over to Spencer lab just now, on my own, but they wouldn't touch it. They refused to take any responsibility for the safekeeping of this dynamite." Lex shook his head. "So I have to take it back to Lincoln again. I'm worried, Cherry."

Cherry brushed strands of her blowing black hair out of her eyes. "Did you tell Dr. Joe you were taking it?"

"No, I didn't want to bother Dr. Joe with such practical matters. I simply was going to tell him that it was safe now."

"Lex," Cherry said in some embarrassment, "you oughtn't to go wandering around with that, without permission, or even without Dr. Joe's knowledge. It—it looks funny. You might be seriously misunderstood."

His face tightened and he looked at her suspiciously. "What's the matter, Cherry, don't you trust me? Did you believe Dr. Wylie's implications the other day?"

"Lex! Don't say such things!" Cherry turned troubled dark eyes on him. "Certainly I trust you. But you have to watch appearances."

"Maybe you don't trust me." He added slowly, "It's surprising how much that hurts."

It hurt Cherry, too. They walked along in a painful tense silence. Cherry suddenly thought of something.

"Lex, do you remember when Dr. Wylie hinted that it was funny you studied up on Dr. Joe's research in order to get the job? Wasn't it the quinine substitute you were working on? And you didn't know about the penicillin, did you?"

Cherry was astounded by Lex's violent reaction to these innocent questions. "So now you, too, are beginning to ask me questions!" he said bitterly.

"Lex!" Cherry cried in amazement. She had meant to tell him that the cleaning woman had gossiped about Dr. Joe's discovery and that the whole hospital was excitedly talking about it. But now she was so distressed she was tongue-tied. Lex's eyes narrowed in anger. They both stood stock-still in the wind, staring at each other. Then with a look of bitterness, he turned on his heel and strode rapidly away.

Lex did not go to the Lincoln Birthday dance. Cherry went. She found she had more attentive doctors and internes for partners than she could dance with. She found, too, from snatches of conversation that evening, that Lex was not so popular in the hospital, after all. "So the uppity Dr. Upham is snubbing us!" they said. "Our dance isn't high-and-mighty enough for him!" Cherry was troubled by such talk.

Meanwhile, Mom was getting rapidly worse. What Cherry had dreaded, happened. Mom had to have another operation, and quickly. And what Cherry had mentioned in joke, also happened. Dr. Wylie was to perform the operation. Mom was old and worn-out and her condition was complicated by still another disorder and a slight cardiac condition. Cherry knew it was serious.

"She has a fifty-fifty chance," Dr. Wylie told the head nurse and Cherry.

The day of the operation she dreaded it as if a member of her own family were to face this ordeal. Only after much pleading, by both Cherry and Mom, had the Superintendent of Nurses consented to let Cherry be present, on her off-duty time, at Mom's operation. She was not to assist, only to watch and hold Mom's hand for encouragement. Cherry thought it was pretty human of the hospital to understand about this, and let her in.

"I'm glad you're with me," Mom whispered to Cherry. They were waiting together in a little anteroom. The O.R. was receiving its last readying touches. "I don't feel alone when I know you're going to be there all the time, Cherry."

"Haven't you any people?" Cherry asked. Mom shook her head.

"I guess I'd better tell you what you call my secret, in case I—go bad on the table," Mom said. She fingered her white operating jacket. "It's this. If anything happens, I don't want my old carcass to go to Potter's Field. Cherry, you fix it up so that won't happen."

Cherry's vision blurred. "I'll fix it, Mom. But nothing's going to happen to you. You're going to come out of this better than you've felt in years."

Mom sighed and groped for Cherry's warm hand. "Maybe it would be just as well if I don't come through it. Because I've been sick a long time and I used up all my savings on hospital bills and I'm most too old to work much any more and I haven't got any place to go and what becomes of old people, anyway?"

"Mom, Mom," Cherry swallowed hard. "You're forgetting we've got a Social Service here in the hospital. They'll send you to some convalescent home in the country and then they'll probably help you apply for your Old Age allowance."

But Mom wasn't convinced. The old lady murmured again, " 'Twould be better if I don't come through. I'm not sure I want to come out of here, not sure at all."

Cherry was terrified. She pleaded with Mom. But Mom only smiled her old gay smile and said, "There, child, don't let yourself get all upset. What'll the surgeon say? No, ma'am, I'll have you laughing in a minute and I'll have that sour old Dr. Wylie laughing, too, if he doesn't watch out."

Cherry smiled shakily. Mom was comforting *her!*

"You know what truly worries me, Cherry?" Mom chuckled. "Why, I haven't got a respectable dress to my name. And that old hat of mine!—I wouldn't wear it to a dog-fight!"

"Get well," Cherry bribed, "and I'll manage to get you some good-looking new clothes."

"I won't be taking anything out of your pocket, honey. Besides," Mom scoffed, "you can't make a fashion plate out of me!"

Cherry squeezed the old lady's hand and followed her as she was wheeled into the Operating Room. Dr. Wylie, accompanied by an assisting interne and the instrument nurse, immediately entered the room. Cherry, who had been holding Mom's hand, dropped it and stepped back out of the way, but not before Dr. Wylie, surprised and apparently annoyed at her presence, glowered at her.

There was an immediate tension felt throughout the room, which communicated itself to Mom. Irrepressible, even now, Mom made an instinctive effort to ease the tension with a wink at the room in general and a hearty "Good night, folks."

"Hypodermic," Dr. Wylie barked at the operating nurse. She administered the morphine. Then Dr. Wylie gave Mom novocain in the affected part. Mom's eyes closed and she grew quiet and relaxed. The nurse gently drew a pad of gauze over Mom's eyes, and Cherry prayed that Mom would drift off to sleep quickly, under the heat of the powerful operating lamp. In any event, Mom would see and hear nothing. The nurse painted the area with iodine. The interne made the incision and quickly clamped and tied off veins and arteries. There was no bleeding. Then, as Dr. Wylie stepped forward and took the scalpel from the nurse, Cherry, who up to this time had been trying to control her emotions—for it was Mom whom she loved who was lying so still on the table—made an audible sound of sympathy. Dr. Wylie, distracted for the moment, turned and gave Cherry a black look.

"Well, Miss Ames!" he observed sarcastically.

Cherry saw the interne and the nurses exchange glances and then look sympathizingly at her over their masks. Embarrassed to the point of tears, Cherry shrank back.

Just then Mom opened her mouth. "Did you know," she said drowsily, "that I'm a sort of nurse myself? Yes, sir, and I—and I nursed in the Spanish-American war, indeed I did. Yes, sir! There was lots of yellow fever and malaria, just like in the Pacific in this war, and I can tell you——"

Dr. Wylie tried to quiet Mom.

But Mom, under the influence of the morphine, chattered on incessantly. "And the bugs! They were something fierce! But we had plenty of quinine," she rambled on, "bugs or no bugs."

Dr. Wylie snapped impatiently, "Miss Ames, you're a friend of this patient's. Perhaps you can justify your presence here by doing something practical. See if you can quiet the patient."

Cherry spoke to Mom but she went right on talking, the words irresponsibly tumbling out. "I read in the newspaper a man right here in this hospital made a quinine substitute. Now, what's that man's name? He's always discovering things . . ."

"Mom!" Cherry said sharply, "keep quiet!" Oh, why had that cleaning woman talked! And to whom else had she talked?

"Fortune, that's his name. Cherry knows him. But Cherry said I mustn't talk about it. It's a secret."

"Mom!" Cherry pleaded, and desperately tried to reach Mom's consciousness. "Mom, you must stop talking, you're disturbing the surgeon."

"A secret, eh?" Dr. Wylie muttered to himself. Cherry wished she could see his face behind that gauze. Oh, this was terrible! What was Dr. Wylie thinking?

"And besides," Mom was talking uncontrollably, "it's a government secret, so it must be pretty important, that new kind of penicillin that this Dr. Fortune's making. The papers say that"—and her voice trailed off, leaving Cherry frozen stiff with terror.

An ominous silence filled the room. Dr. Wylie proceeded with the operation. "Nurse! Suture!" he curtly demanded. The nurse handed him a suture, a tie, a sponge.

Once Mom turned her head and said vaguely, "Cherry? Are you still there?"

"I'm right here, Mom," Cherry reassured her in a stifled voice.

Dr. Wylie finished. "She'll be all right," he said. There was a note of pity in his voice. Then abruptly he turned to Cherry, "I would like to see you alone, Miss Ames."

Frightened and quaking, Cherry started to follow, when suddenly the young interne unexpectedly came to her defense. "May I say one thing, sir? What the old lady just said is common gossip around the hospital." Dr. Wylie glared at him, then stormed out. There was nothing for Cherry to do but follow his stiff, unyielding back out of the Operating Room. "Now!" thought Cherry . . .

Alone, he faced Cherry and exclaimed, "So you can't keep a secret! You had to talk!"

"No, sir!" She explained rapidly how the cleaning woman in all innocence had divulged the secret.

Dr. Wylie brushed her explanation aside. "I don't care for that young Upham! If Fortune doesn't choose his assistants more carefully than that, perhaps the hospital had better take away his research grant!"

Cherry was nearly in tears. Dr. Wylie could turn them all out of the hospital—Dr. Joe, Lex, Cherry—with a blackened professional reputation besides! He might even, for the sake of safety, send Mom away at once . . . poor Mom, who needed help so urgently.

"It's not this old lady's fault, sir," Cherry pleaded. "Please don't penalize her. She's alone and penniless and she has to have help. And I hardly think it's Dr. Upham's fault, either. I know him well and I think he is . . ."

"You think! You think! Can't you understand the military importance of this new drug? Good heavens, we're fighting a war!" With a gesture of resignation, he turned abruptly on his heel and strode away.

Cherry, still trembling with fear, went back to see how Mom was coming along. Mom had been calling for her.

"You'll be all right," Cherry told Mom softly. "Now just go to sleep and I'll be here taking care of you. And for heaven's sake don't talk any more!"

"Why, did I say anything?" Mom asked with incredulous round eyes. "I was asleep! I didn't say a word!"

"You talked about Dr. Joe's penicillin!"

"Good heavens! Cherry! What've I done? If anything happens to it, it'd be my fault!"

Back at work, Cherry was too busy to worry about the safety of the drug, or what Dr. Wylie thought. That would have to take care of itself, while she encouraged Mom to get well.

But Mom would not cooperate. She never again said she did not want to live. But Cherry saw her lying staring into space with empty eyes. She knew Mom was brooding about facing a bleak future the moment she was discharged from the hospital. She knew, too, that Mom felt deeply guilty for betraying the secret of the drug. Outside, sharp March winds were blowing the snow away, but even the coming of spring did not cheer up Mom—jokes, flowers, a surprise on her tray— nothing helped. Then Cherry remembered her promise to get Mom some presentable clothes. She sensed, too, Mom's unwillingness to be dependent.

Cherry got back to Crowley late one night, and she had barely stamped the ice and wet off her overshoes when she got her savings bank book out of the desk. It was not enough She could not afford to outfit Mom alone. Cherry got a piece of paper and a pencil. She started to write down a list of Mom's friends here in the hospital.

During the next two weeks, Cherry tramped from one building to another, knocked on doors, left notes in letter boxes, spoke to staff people on the floor of her ward, talked on the phone. "It's for Mom?" they all asked. "Certainly!" By the end of that time, sixty people had contributed various sums.

It was Friday evening. Mom was to be discharged on Saturday morning, tomorrow morning. She was being sent to a convalescent farm for elderly people, a few miles out of the city. Mom did not want to go. She was pathetically silent on the subject of her future and would talk only of things which were safely in the past. Just now she was across the hall in the neighboring ward, saying good-by to the nurses and patients in there.

"Now!" Cherry said, and the four nurses on the floor, who had appointed themselves as her committee, brought out the boxes which Cherry had smuggled in that afternoon. They opened them, and everyone marveled at how Cherry had stretched the money. The patients in their beds looked on in curiosity, and nurses and internes stuck their heads in the door to watch. There was a good deal of eager, whispered advice and giggling, and then a hushed excitement as Mom's voice approached in the corridor.

Mom stood in the doorway, leaning on a cane. Her eyes grew big as she saw what was on her bed. At first she could only stand and stare, and look questioningly from one smiling face to another.

"It's for—for *me?*" she asked carefully. She clutched her checkered kimono about her and hurried as best she could to the bed. There lay a blue dress, a black dress, a warm black coat, a pretty hat, shoes and stockings, underthings, gloves, everything Mom could need.

Mom gasped. She pressed her hands to her heart. "Well, I never!" she said in awestruck tones. She tentatively put out a shaking hand, as if to see if the clothes were real. She turned to Cherry, trying to smile. "I'm going to walk out of here in style! Why, I can't wait to put 'em on and show 'em off!" Suddenly she bent her head and wept.

"I'm an old fool to be crying," she declared, wiping her eyes. "But you're—all so—good to me!"

"Look inside the purse, Mom," someone suggested. The old lady was so excited they had to tell her two or three times. At last she opened the purse with trembling hands. There were two crisp bills and shining new coins.

"Oh me, oh my!" Mom dissolved into tears again. She tugged desperately at her braids. "Cherry, I bet you did this!"

"We all wanted to give you a going-away present," Cherry said gently. "Here's a list of all your friends who hope you like these."

Just then there was a well-known gruff and impatient voice in the hall. It was Dr. Wylie coming to give Mom a final check-up before giving his permission that she be discharged. Cherry had completely forgotten he was coming. What would he think when he saw her extra-curricular activities? Cherry wanted to sweep the clothes out of sight but there was no time. On top of all her other serious difficulties with him, now this!

He marched directly to Mom, ignoring the nurses and internes who were rejoicing with Mom. They scattered in fright, as if he had swept them out of the way. "Step over here," he ordered Mom. "Pull the curtains, nurse."

Cherry drew the white duck curtains around Mom's bed, making it a little private unit in the ward. Dr. Wylie did not so much as speak to Cherry. He examined Mom painstakingly and his cold eyes swept over the new garments. "Satisfactory," he pronounced. "Miss Ames, I want to speak to you in the corridor. Alone."

"Yes, doctor," she said.

"Here it comes!" Cherry thought. She followed him with reluctant feet out into the corridor. Two nurses who were chatting there saw Dr. Wylie coming and parted hastily.

"Miss Ames!"

"Yes, Dr. Wylie."

He fixed his steely gaze on her vivid face. Cherry was sure he was making mental note of "that rouge" he stubbornly insisted she wore.

"Harrumph! About that clothing, Miss Ames."

"Yes, sir."

"Word that you were taking up a collection reached my ears." Cherry quaked at his stern tone. Had she done something unauthorized? Had she broken some strict hospital rule? Maybe this infraction was serious enough for suspension, or even expulsion! "I presume you did it with good intentions and that the patient needs assistance."

"Yes, sir," Cherry said faintly.

"Don't interrupt me! You always were a cheeky young woman." He cleared his throat and glared at her. "I was about to say that I should like to contribute also." Dr. Wylie whipped out a checkbook and a fountain pen. Cherry stood there gaping. He wrote out a check for a very substantial sum.

"Thank you, Dr. Wylie, thank you! This will do wonders for her!"

"I didn't ask you what it will do, did I?" Dr. Wylie was embarrassed, and so, gruffer than ever. "See that you go with her to a bank tomorrow so she can cash it. And something else, Miss Ames."

Cherry hardly dared breathe.

"I've arranged for employment for her, here at the hospital, when she returns. She is to supervise the cleaning staff in—er—Lincoln Hall. She will—er—have a key."

Lincoln Hall! That meant Dr. Wylie forgave Mom for blabbing about the secret drug! He was saying publicly that he trusted her. So Dr. Wylie saw Mom's worth. How generous of him this was!

Cherry said gratefully, "Mom has been feeling dreadfully guilty about mentioning the penicillin when she was under anaesthetic."

"This gossip is not her fault," Dr. Wylie said tersely. "Good night, Miss Ames."

"Good night, sir," Cherry smiled.

She stood there a moment looking at the slip of paper—to Louella Barker from Lewis Wylie. To an obscure, helpless old lady from one of the most famous surgeons in the country—via a student nurse who loved and believed in nursing.

CHAPTER XI

Three Letters

GETTING UP AT SIX WASN'T SO BAD, CHERRY THOUGHT, as the rising bell clanged and she staggered from bed onto her feet. It was waking up that was the hard part. She groped blindly out into the hall of Crowley, avoided bumping into the other sleepy chattering nurses, and somehow found her way to the shower. Then she staggered back to her room and pulled on her uniform and apron. She sleep-walked across the yard, sniffing at the hint of spring in the cold rainy air, and blinked her way into the nurses' dining room.

"Good morning," said Gwen, from the table near the door. The redheaded girl was offensively wide-awake and cheerful over her bowl of cereal. "Did you ever see such a dripping morning?"

"It's a morning for sleeping," moaned Ann, looming up in the doorway. "Come on, Cherry." The two girls took their trays and went up to the food counter. They brought their breakfasts back to Gwen's table. Bertha and Mai Lee showed up, too, crisp and fresh in their blue and white.

"What a day!" Bertha said. "Well, this April rain will soften up the ground for spring planting."

Cherry yawned and tried to take an interest in her omelet.

Gwen cleared her throat. "I have a letter from Miss Mac," she announced innocently.

Cherry suddenly woke up. "Miss McIntyre? Our old nursing arts instructor?" All the girls had adored that lively, dashing young woman, who had volunteered a year ago as an Army nurse.

"Welcome to our midst, Cherry," Gwen grinned. "Nice to have you conscious again."

"Stop stalling!" all the others insisted. "Read it!"

Gwen pulled the letter out of her apron pocket. It was addressed to the entire class and postmarked Africa. It was packed with excitement and Miss Mac's contagious gaiety. ". . . two thousand men and us thirty nurses on that ship, and was it exciting. . . . There we were in North Africa. . . . That was the first time I heard guns . . . cold here in Africa sometimes. We wear dungarees and boots, and we do each other's hair. The soldiers call us 'angels in long underwear' . . . the bravest, nicest bunch of boys I ever knew. And there they lie. They're so grateful for the least little thing we nurses do for them . . . how we nurses drill. You ought to see us run for cover and throw ourselves flat in foxholes. The soldiers say we're good . . . can't wait to get well so they can get right back and fight . . . exotic towns here, curious food, veiled women, necklaces of beaten silver. We washed our stockings in a river they say stems from the Nile . . . such a romantic officer and we're Army lieutenants ourselves, you know. . . ."

Far places, adventure, danger, action—Cherry's breath came faster.

"Some of the things I see are pretty sad . . . nurses are badly needed. There aren't nearly enough . . . here is where you can put to good use all the training you have had . . . and here is where you feel that at last you are really useful. Our boys do need you, so won't you please come?"

Gwen passed the letter on to the next table. The girls sat there in silence. Then Ann lifted her head.

"I know you kids don't want to ask me, so I'll tell you. Bill and Gerry—my kid brothers—are in Army training camps out West. But Jack—" Ann unpinned a silk change purse from her apron pocket and took out a small, brilliant diamond ring. It was the first time she showed it to anyone. Ann said in an expressionless voice, "Jack's been shipped out. All I know is that he's somewhere in the Pacific. And it's going to be a long war."

"Annie," Mai Lee said, trying to sound casual, "we'll enlist in the Nurse Corps together."

"It's a date," Ann tried to smile. She stood up suddenly. "I have to run." She disappeared, looking very sober.

Cherry said thoughtfully, "I had letters, too, this morning. One from my brother Charlie and one from my mother. If you'll excuse me, I'll go into the library and read them."

Charlie's letter was terse, determined, right to the point—like himself. It was written from an Army Air Force training field in Texas. He had enlisted this winter and now he had successfully completed his training as an aerial gunner. "At first they wanted me to be a chauffeur—pilot to you—but I think this job is more important, defending the plane and crew so the bombardier can get there and drop his eggs. Then they argued I was too tall for the gunner's nest. But I knew what I wanted to do. Now I'm all set to go upstairs. Our crew is a fine bunch of men, we stick together like brothers. Our plane is quite a baby, a four-motor B-17 with a wing spread almost a block long. This will be the last letter I'll write you from this base. Can't give you any address, yet. We're going out soon. Don't know where, but anywhere we can eliminate a few Nazis is all right with me. Glad you're enjoying the perfume. Don't worry about me."

Don't worry, he said! Cherry thought wryly she had better do something more constructive than worry. For the first time, it seriously occurred to her that she could become an Army nurse. But what about her decision to nurse here at home? She frowned. This was going to be a hard choice to make. The restlessness surged up in her, stronger than it had ever been. Confused, she turned her mind instead to her mother's letter. The firm but delicate handwriting was comfortingly familiar:

"Hilton is so changed. . . . That little old airfield at Wabash City is being enlarged, and is teeming with Army men. Wouldn't it be wonderful if Charlie could be stationed there? But I guess that won't happen. . . . Dad is very busy these days. He spends more time selling war bonds than real estate. Dad and Midge help me with our Victory garden. . . . Midge and I are going to put up cherries and corn as soon as the first crop is in, and this summer we will can vegetables. It will save our ration points. Midge is a great comfort to have around in this empty house, but I must admit she is a handful too. . . . The clinic here has asked me to be a nurse's aide and I am going to see if I can't make the time for it. Midge wants so badly to be a nurse's aide. . . . We had another air-raid drill two nights ago. We sat in the dark most of the evening and the puppy barked the whole time. . . . Well, dear, this is all for now. Keep yourself well, and try to have some recreation. . . ."

That showed Cherry nurses were needed at home, too. Home front? War front? Which sort of nurse was she to be? She started off for her ward, thinking hard.

~~~~~~

CHAPTER XII

Madame Zaza

AFTER THOSE LETTERS, CHERRY FOUND CONTAGIOUS Ward boring. When she thought of what Miss Mac was doing, all these isolation techniques and anti-contamination techniques seemed tiresome. Of course it was important to keep diseases from spreading, for an epidemic could take as many lives as a battle. It was important to learn how to protect herself and other patients. But Cherry was heartily sick of all this painstaking routine; sick of scrubbing herself endlessly after touching contaminated linen or dishes; of burning germ-laden matter and then scrubbing again; of remembering to turn her face away from the patient, remembering at every move to take precautions lest she carry diphtheria or pneumonia or typhoid germs out of the sickroom with her, and infect others.

April dragged along. Cherry was working away quietly one afternoon in Dr. Joe's laboratory. She missed Lex dreadfully. Since their last bitter conversation, Lex made it a point to be out of the laboratory when Cherry was likely to be there. It made Cherry feel very badly, but she determined to let Lex sulk it out.

"What was wrong with everybody, anyway?" Cherry wondered. Even Dr. Joe didn't look his usual absent-minded self. Dr. Joe was worried about something.

When Dr. Joe looked up from his microscope, Cherry listened to him anxiously. "Cherry," he said, "Dr. Wylie's leave came to an end today and he has left for the front." Then with a worried frown, he continued, "Before he went he had a talk with me . . . alone. He was very much annoyed. The whole hospital is talking about the drug—news has somehow leaked out. Dr. Wylie can be a very stern disciplinarian, as you know." Cherry nodded. She remembered only too well what he had threatened at Mom's operation. Dr. Joe continued, "He has insisted that I take more precautions about safeguarding the drug or else . . ."

"Are you doing that?" asked Cherry.

Dr. Joe looked at her helplessly. "Somehow, child, I don't seem to be able to think of practical things!"

"But you must, Dr. Joe!" Cherry warned. "You do want to send this new penicillin synthesis to the battle areas, don't you? You said it's even more urgent than the quinine. Please be careful with it, Dr. Joe," Cherry pleaded. "You must! Especially now that the whole hospital is gossiping about it!"

"I'll be careful," he promised. "But I can't understand how word leaked out . . . " Cherry started to tell him about the cleaning woman, but Dr. Joe had turned back to his table, and was bending over the microscope, already absorbedly interested in what he was studying. Cherry, knowing that he had completely forgotten her presence, shook her head hopelessly and walked dejectedly out of the room.

Cherry had more than just the worry for the safety of Dr. Joe's new drug on her mind these days. She was constantly being reminded of the crying need for medical care in the battle zones, and her restlessness grew. Everywhere she looked the urgency of war nursing confronted her. New probationers were coming in now and more than half of them were going to complete their training in twenty-six to thirty months, instead of the usual three years, and their total expenses were to be paid by the U.S. Cadet Nurse Corps.

On the other hand, more and more nurses and doctors were streaming out of Spencer Hospital for the battle fronts. There had been a farewell party for a dozen of them only last week. The shortage of nurses was already acute and Cherry knew that as the war progressed, this condition would grow worse. She fully realized the dire need for nurses on the war front, and at the same time, she could not erase from her mind the picture of all those helpless patients, right here, who needed nursing care. Torn between the two, Cherry worriedly debated where she would be of more service after graduation—on the home front? or on the war front?

Cherry ached to talk her problems over with Lex, but he was still avoiding her and she was too proud and too stubborn to seek him out.

So Cherry did not consult Lex, and decided the best thing she could do was to get along with her studies.

The senior class was now having lectures on neurology and psychiatry which would continue throughout May. Cherry learned that just as people's bodies became ill, so did their minds. In studying case histories, Cherry summoned up enough imagination to understand what was going on in those injured minds, those twisted emotions. And, not surprisingly, all this gave her a clue to Mildred's mixed-up attitude.

She seemed to understand a little better, now, that Mildred was afraid, and probably starved for affection. But her lack of self-confidence blocked her ability to give and receive affection. What the cause of this "emotional blockage" was, Cherry did not know and could not guess. This fear, which Mildred made up for by pretending boldness and indifference, might have stemmed from her unattractive appearance, or from the fact that she was only a mediocre student. But Cherry did not honestly understand, and at any rate she had made her decision. She was going to see Miss Reamer.

It was a lovely afternoon at the very end of May, when Cherry at last found time to go to Miss Reamer's office. Tender new leaves blew on the trees, filmy clouds drifted across a light blue sky. It was too beautiful a day for such an unpleasant task. Nevertheless, Cherry marched firmly into the Superintendent's office.

Miss Reamer was in her inner private office, seated behind a desk. She looked capable and dignified in her white nurse's uniform. She welcomed Cherry and asked what she had come to discuss.

Cherry recounted to her, just as they had happened, her difficulties with her adoptee. She made it clear that Mildred was a conscientious student, a responsible member of the School, and got along smoothly, if not very cordially, with other students and staff members. Miss Reamer listened in silence. When Cherry had finished, she said coldly:

"So you've failed!"

Cherry was startled. She hardly knew what to say. "But I tried—I tried my very best."

"No, you did not, Miss Ames. You and I have discussed this several times before, and I warned you it was your own fault. I know Miss Burnham. She is rather difficult. But so are a great many people. It's possible—

as well as necessary, especially for a nurse—to find the right ways to deal with them. But it takes a great deal of understanding and patience, and that must be where you failed."

That was what Mom had said. Cherry tried to estimate honestly the effort she had made with Mildred. It seemed to her she had made her maximum effort. "It's true I don't understand Mildred," she admitted to Miss Reamer. "I've come to certain conclusions about her"—she told the Superintendent what she thought—"but I don't know how accurately that describes her."

Miss Reamer nodded. "I think that's very accurate. Mildred wants to be friends with you—she showed you that when she made a birthday gift for you—but she doesn't really know how to be friends. Yes, I think you do understand Mildred. But I think—as I've said before—that you've been intolerant and impatient with her. I suspect, Miss Ames, that when you believed you were thinking about Mildred, you were really thinking of reasons to justify your own attitude."

Cherry felt a sharp pang of shame. Miss Reamer was right. Cherry had wrestled with her own intolerance, and instead of facing it, here she was trying to escape and excuse herself.

The older woman smiled at her. "I have had several talks with Mildred, on routine matters, and she has never failed to express her gratitude and admiration for you." Cherry was astonished. "Yes, really," Miss Reamer said. "You see, Mildred thought you didn't like her—and you didn't. You hurt her. That's what caused all your trouble." She smiled comfortingly. "Don't feel so badly. You've really had quite a problem to handle there. Do you still want to give up?"

Cherry flushed. "I'd like to try again. But how shall I start?"

Miss Reamer pushed her chair back from the desk, and considered. She said slowly, "First, you must really like her. Your mind has been working on this problem, but your heart hasn't. Then you must realize that Mildred likes you—you've been cagey and defensive yourself, you know." Cherry remembered how she had curbed her enthusiasm when she wrote the note congratulating Mildred on winning her cap. "I wager, Miss Ames, that if you give Mildred the chance, she will *prove* her devotion to you! And then—" Miss Reamer frowned, thinking "—you must be friendly enough for two. Why don't you ask Mildred to have dinner downtown with you and spend the evening doing something you'd both enjoy—see a show or you can shop on certain evenings or attend a radio broadcast or take a boat ride up the river. A change from the hospital atmosphere might help. And do it several times. You can't help liking people with whom you have pleasant times."

Cherry listened to these suggestions eagerly. Then her face fell. "Mildred will refuse. She always refuses my invitations."

Miss Reamer threw back her gray head and laughed. "Then insist. Put her hat and coat on her, and take her by the hand. I assure you, she's longing to be asked!"

Cherry got to her feet, feeling much better. "Thank you, Miss Reamer," she said, and Cherry was genuinely grateful for her understanding help. She went off immediately to see Mildred. She realized both she and Mildred were on trial—a trial of good will.

She knocked on Mildred's door. Her adoptee's room was on the ground floor of the residence hall for first-year and junior students, which faced Lincoln Hall. Mildred let her in, looking puzzled.

"Change your dress and put on your hat and meet me in the rotunda in ten minutes!" Cherry announced. Her black eyes were dancing. This was going to be fun, at that.

"What? Why?" Mildred looked at her suspiciously.

"Because it's such beautiful weather, we're going on a spree! We're going out for dinner and then I've some grand ideas for the evening. Hurry up!"

Mildred mumbled something about having to study, but Cherry's high spirits were catching. "If you don't show up, I'll come and get you!" Cherry told her. Mildred looked bewildered but pleased.

Ten minutes later Cherry arrived at the rotunda, in a red wool suit, her cheeks red with excitement, a tiny red cap on her black curls. There was Mildred, waiting for her, dressed in her very best, looking expectant. Miss Reamer was right!

"It *is* too nice to stay in and study," Mildred justified herself.

"Anyone who studies in this spring weather is plumb crazy—no, I shouldn't say that," Cherry laughed. "If you get stuck on today's lesson, we'll cram on it—by flashlight, if necessary."

Mildred looked amused and began to be more at ease.

"Let's blow ourselves," Cherry said suddenly. "Let's buy ourselves flowers, to start with." Mildred looked incredulous, but she tagged along eagerly with Cherry to the florist's. Cherry chose one huge flat red and white camellia to go with her suit, and Mildred had a lovely time trying to decide between some tiny roses and spicy carnations. The florist wearily suggested that she toss a coin, but it was Cherry who came to the rescue.

"Look, here's a favorite French way." She picked up three pink carnations and three white ones, and massed the heads together into a solid round ball, pink on one side and white on the other. Mildred looked on, fascinated. The florist cut off the stems. "No ribbons," Cherry said. "There, my love," and she pinned the nosegay on Mildred's blue coat. Mildred stood on tiptoe to admire herself in the florist's high mirror. She was pleased and amazed.

"Where did you learn to do that?" she asked Cherry as they went out onto the street.

"Ah, I am Madame ZaZa, sees all, knows all."

Mildred giggled. "What else can you see?"

"Madame ZaZa she see a taxi. Come weeth ZaZa, my leetle carnation!" And they sprang into a taxi. They giggled and talked nonsense all the beautiful ride downtown along the river.

They splurged on sodas, window shopped till their eyes bugged out, then enjoyed a leisurely luscious Italian dinner. Both girls were enjoying themselves, and the old tension dropped away as if by magic. They talked of everything under the sun. For a while they talked about Mom; Cherry had been writing her encouraging letters at the convalescent farm. Then Mildred mentioned the new penicillin drug and repeated some of the gossip that was going on around the hospital.

"You know Dr. Fortune, don't you?" Mildred suddenly asked.

"Yes, all my life. Sometimes I help him in his laboratory."

"Cherry," Mildred said awkwardly and fell silent. Cherry wondered what was coming. "Maybe this will sound silly. And maybe all this gossip is making my imagination run away with me. But strange things seem to be going on in Dr. Fortune's lab late at night. Last night, from my window, I saw lights going on and off, almost as if someone were sending signals with a flashlight."

Cherry instantly became alert, but she remembered that she must guard her tongue.

"Oh, Dr. Joe likes to work at night," she said casually and a little indifferently.

Noting Cherry's seeming lack of interest, Mildred said, "Well, maybe it *was* imagination. But I thought you'd be interested."

"I am interested," Cherry said quietly. "If you see anything strange up there, please tell me *immediately.*" She made a mental note to see Dr. Joe early the next morning. And with that mental reservation made, she proceeded to enjoy the evening's fun.

They were so heavy with good food after leaving the restaurant that they simply needed a walk. They strolled along the river's edge, watching the water and boats and the opposite shore grow deeper and deeper blue in the dusk.

Out of the romantic leafy shadows, Mildred announced, "I'm hungry."

"You can't be!"

"Well, I am."

"Let's have another soda," Cherry suggested. "What's one mere soda on a spree?"

The sodas turned into large and substantial sundaes. The two girls sauntered out of the shop and found a movie theater next door, showing a picture about Army nurses.

"What could be more perfect!" Cherry sighed. "But we'd better sit in the balcony—our funds are melting away."

The seats which they found in the darkened house were at least a block away from the screen. But they had a fine time. When they came out, Cherry looked at her wrist watch and gasped.

"It's almost ten! Oh, my gosh! Do you think we'll get back to sign in on time—even with a taxi?"

"Can we afford a taxi?" Mildred asked desperately. They opened their purses and hastily compared resources. They could just afford it.

They urged the driver on to an unlawful speed and kept peering at Cherry's watch. "Madame ZaZa," said Mildred with a straight face, "if you know all, why didn't you know it was getting late?"

That set them off into a fit of laughter. They were still laughing when they raced out of the taxi, and signed in on the perilous dot of ten.

"Good night," Mildred said in the dark hospital yard. "I liked it. Let's do it again soon."

"As soon as we have a few cents in our jeans again," Cherry promised. "Good night, Carnation." She went off to Crowley feeling warmly satisfied. This was the best time, the first really successful time, she had ever had with her adoptee. She was beginning to like Mildred now. And apparently Mildred liked her.

Cherry tumbled into bed and fell asleep before she could say "Mildred Burnham." She was full of fresh air and spaghetti and chocolate pecan sundae, and she slept like a baby.

She was deep in dreams when an insistent knocking at her door awakened her. Cherry blinked. It was still deep night, soundless except for the rustle of trees in the yard, and the knocking.

"Go away!" Cherry called.

"Telephone!" came a nurse's muffled voice.

Cherry crawled out of bed and groped for her slippers and robe. "Didn't hear a thing," she said to the sleepy nurse, who had the room at the end of the hall where the phone was located. "I'm sorry you were wakened on my account," Cherry managed to say sleepily. "What time is it?"

"Ten minutes after four," the nurse yawned and went back into her room.

Four o'clock . . . ten minutes after . . . what was wrong? Cherry picked up the dangling receiver.

"Cherry! this is Dr. Joe! My new drug—my penicillin synthesis—it's gone!"

CHAPTER XIII

Lex Is Proven

TWO EXTRAORDINARY THINGS HAPPENED TO CHERRY IN June. She was questioned by detectives, Army Intelligence and F.B.I. men. She was made a student head nurse and put in charge of a ward.

The investigators did not get very far in discovering who had stolen Dr. Joe's drug. The thief had taken not only the drug but part of the highly complicated formula. Fortunately the second page of it had been in Dr. Joe's pocket that night. Cherry wondered if the thief might sometime return for that second page. The F.B.I. posted a guard, day and night, around Lincoln Hall. But the thief made no further effort to obtain the rest of the formula. Cherry grew used to seeing the plainclothesmen around Lincoln Hall, though few others knew who they were. The questioning was over, the talk about the crime died down. Even Dr. Joe kept a resigned unhappy silence. Everything was peaceful again, on the surface.

The affair had one heartbreaking aftermath, at least half of the hospital suspected Lex. Several facts pointed to Lex's possible guilt: he and Dr. Joe possessed the only two keys to the laboratory, and he was evasive and kept sullenly to himself. Dr. Joe ignored the gossip and kept Lex on at his laboratory. But Lex still avoided meeting Cherry there.

The bright June morning when Cherry went in as student head nurse on Men's Surgical convalescent ward, the supervisor said, with obvious distaste:

"I want you to meet the doctor who will work with you these three months on this ward." The door opened and the supervisor said ironically, "Dr. Upham."

Lex and Cherry stared at each other. They would have to work together daily, whether or not they wanted to see each other!

Lex said stiffly, "I congratulate you, Miss Ames, on being one of the few in the senior class to merit the post of student head nurse."

It was painful making the rounds of the patients, walking side by side with Lex daily, talking only when it was necessary. Lex looked thin and worried these days. In her heart Cherry knew that he was too decent to have had even the smallest part in such sordid business. But all around her people were shunning Lex, whispering about him and surrounding him in such an ugly atmosphere of suspicion that Cherry did not know what to think!

Little doubtful thoughts began to bother her. Why was Lex being so evasive and aloof? Also nagging away at the back of her mind was that scene in the laboratory when Lex told her he needed money but emphatically refused to tell her why. There was gossip, too, about how Cherry and Lex had quarreled because of the theft and it was said that Cherry had dropped Lex because she thought he was guilty. Nothing of the sort was true. But Lex heard this talk, and believed it. Cherry would have been glad to try to straighten out these lies. But Lex, taking the gossip seriously, kept her at arm's length with the professional formality of a doctor to a nurse.

"I wish I'd never been made a student head nurse!" Cherry said miserably to Gwen one day after Lex had walked out, coldly aloof as ever.

"Never mind, Lex will be cleared yet," Gwen said stoutly. Gwen had not been assigned to a head nurse post, but she said she did not mind, for she had had so much experience of this kind helping her doctor father. "I hate executive work, anyway," she had told Cherry and Ann.

Cherry had no dislike for the work, but no particular liking for it either. It meant being ward planner and policeman over Gwen, another senior whom she barely knew, and two anxious first-year students. Cherry's four subordinates worked under her willingly and pleasantly. It was quite a responsibility, seeing that twenty-three men in varying stages of health after operations received efficient care. There were smaller, nagging responsibilities, too, like seeing that the laundry went out and got back on time; that the first-year nurses' mistakes were prevented or caught in time; that Dr. Upham's orders were carried out; that special foods and drugs needed on the ward were requisitioned; that the endless reports and records were kept accurately. There were dozens of things which Cherry had to supervise, coordinate and organize, so that the ward would run smoothly. Besides this, Cherry was having classes in public health nursing and in ethics. It was a heavy program.

Cherry was quite a good manager, but she had two difficulties. One was her own lateness, which two or three times tangled up the ward schedule. Another was her unwillingness to discipline her nurses, especially when she could see that they were tired. She remembered only too vividly how she had felt when she was a ward nurse. However, when Cherry made an effort to be on time and forced herself to become a little stricter with her nurses, her detailed reports to the supervisor showed an improvement in how the ward was being managed.

Also on her mind these summer days was where she was going to nurse—here at home or on the war front.

The term was nearly over, graduation loomed very close. She *must* decide, and soon.

In July the heat became oppressive and Cherry's whole ward was moved out to canvas pavilions in the yard. It was pleasant working outdoors, especially in the fragrant summer evenings. But even summertime did not soften Lex's attitude. His and Cherry's tense, painful daily routine continued. The accusing gossip about Lex continued. The detectives had neither found the drug thief nor had they uncovered any clues. Dr. Joe was struggling to work out again the first, stolen page of the formula. Cherry received an anxious letter from Midge, asking her to keep an eye on her father.

"I wish I could do something for Dr. Joe and for Lex, both," Cherry told Ann and Gwen. "They're close to the breaking point."

"I keep thinking of what the loss means to all those sick and wounded soldiers," Ann said. "Oh, what's the use of talking about it?"

"It doesn't look," Gwen said, "as if Dr. Joe is going to get it back."

Cherry was forced to agree. She had thought and thought, until her mind ached, about how she could help. There were so many people working in this huge hospital, so many patients, so many visitors, delivery men—out of several thousand people, and no clues, it was nearly hopeless to sift out the criminal. Government authorities ordered the story kept out of the newspapers, but it was common knowledge around the hospital that the thief had made a successful getaway. It was enough to embolden him to a second attempt. Cherry was furious, depressed, and hopeless. She felt it was only a question of time before gossip would drive Lex from the hospital and Dr. Joe would be dismissed.

It was with affairs in this state that Mom returned to Spencer, and her new job. Cherry went down to the train to meet her. The old lady was in good health now and elated about her job. She was to be in charge of the cleaning women at Lincoln Hall. She even had a key to Lincoln Hall.

"But there's one thing I ought to tell you," Cherry said as they rode back to the hospital. "There are F.B.I. men in and around Lincoln all the time."

"F.B.I. men! G-men!" Mom exclaimed. "Oh, I see They're there to make sure no one steals the drug."

"To tell you the truth," Cherry said reluctantly, "the drug has been stolen." She told Mom the details of what had happened.

Tears stood in Mom's eyes. "It's my fault! I—talked! Don't say otherwise, Cherry. If it hadn't been for me, blabbing——"

Cherry did her best to assure Mom that this was not so. But Mom could not be convinced. She felt horribly guilty and vowed that she would do anything she could to recover the drug.

"Cheer up, Mom," Cherry said finally. "I have one nice thing to tell you. There was a vacant room in Crowley and I got it for you."

"Well, that's nice," Mom said, "but that drug—it is my fault—I've got to make up for it."

Cherry tried, on succeeding days, to lighten Mom's terrible burden of guilt. But Mom seemed to have an obsession on the subject.

Cherry herself tried to stop worrying by watching another influx of beginning students. Spencer Hospital, like many other hospitals, now had three terms a year because of the war emergency, so that students could enter in the fall, spring, or summer. Cherry was glad and relieved to see these new seventeen- and eighteen-year old girls. She certainly could use an extra probationer on her own ward. Yet out of all this flow of nurses, Cherry saw that there were still not enough of them. Fortunately the U.S. Cadet Nurse Corps was opening the gates to nursing wider than they had ever been opened before.

Cherry went to bed early one night. It was hot. She had had a long, difficult day. Outside in the yard there were lively voices and footsteps for a while, then silence. Yet Cherry had difficulty in falling asleep. She could not explain an uneasiness which pervaded her. When she did sleep, it was a heavy fitful slumber. She woke from it more tired than before. Her clock said one. She turned the pillow over, and buried her warm face in the cool linen. The hot thick air was so still, the leaves outside hung motionless. You could hear a pin drop a block away on a night like this, Cherry thought, and drifted back to sleep.

Later on, much later on, Cherry became aware that someone was in her room. She could see a black figure outlined against the shadowy wall. Her breath came fast and hard. She wanted to scream, but she found her throat was too tightened to utter a sound.

"Sh! Don't be frightened, it's only me—Mildred." She was panting as if she had been running. "I didn't dare knock or make a sound. Don't raise your voice."

Cherry sat up, sharply awake. "What's happened?"

Cherry could hear Mildred swallow hard before she was able to speak again. "There's a light—in Dr. Fortune's lab! I saw a man silhouetted up there—just for a moment. His flashlight keeps going on and off, in the same spot. Detectives or watchmen don't behave like that. And Dr. Fortune—well, it's not Dr. Fortune because he'd turn on all the lights. And—and, Cherry—" She clung to Cherry's arm with cold hands. "There's a man watching on the north side of Lincoln. He's hiding in the doorway. And he doesn't look like a watchman or a detective." She leaned against Cherry, trembling. Cherry put her arm around the girl.

"But, Mildred, why did you take such a risk? You left your building—he could have seen you—*must* have seen you! What a dangerous thing for you to do! He could have tried to stop you. Why didn't you phone me?"

"I didn't *think* of the telephone. When I saw the light all I could think of was getting to you as fast as I could."

"But how did you get past your supervisor?"

"She doesn't know where I am," said Mildred. "I didn't ask for permission—I was afraid she wouldn't let me go. And they may leave any minute!"

"Brave girl!" Cherry whispered back. She got out of bed and found her shoes and clothes. "What are we going to do? We've got to let the police know. Thank goodness the F.B.I. man is over there." Cherry suddenly stopped dressing. "Mildred, perhaps something has happened to him—he may be in danger. We mustn't let them get away! Come on!"

They stepped softly out into the corridor. "I'm going with you," Mildred whispered. "I won't let you go into that dangerous place alone. Don't argue, there isn't time. What are you doing?"

Cherry quickly and quietly entered Gwen's room, a few doors down, and woke her. Gwen shook the sleep out of her eyes and listened.

"Go get Ann," Cherry said very low. "Don't make a sound. Somebody's up to something in Dr. Fortune's laboratory. Give us ten minutes to get over to Lincoln.

Then call the police. Tell them there's a lookout on the north side door. Got it? And hurry. Mildred and I will try to stall them there one way or another until the police get here."

"Okay," Gwen whispered. She already had her shoes on and stood up. "But don't get yourselves killed! Got flashlights? Here, Mildred, you take mine."

Cherry saw Gwen open Ann's door. Cherry went to her own night supervisor's office. It was empty. The supervisor must be making her rounds. But she could not wait for her to return. She and Mildred dashed down to Mom's room.

Cherry gently opened Mom's door. "Mom, wake up!" She shook her. "Mom, wake up!"

The old lady blinked and raised herself on one elbow. "Why, Cherry, honey, what do you want at this hour of the night?"

Cherry rapidly explained. "I want you to give me the key to Lincoln Hall."

"The key to Lincoln!" Mom's mouth stayed open. "But the F.B.I. man——"

"Exactly," Cherry whispered firmly. "I'm sure something has happened in Lincoln. We've got to get in there somehow. You want to get the drug back, don't you?"

"I sure do! I'd do anything to make up for my blabbing." Mom grabbed the key from the purse under her pillow and thrust it at Cherry.

"But what are you going to do, child? How are you going to keep them there?"

"I don't know yet," said Cherry. "I'll think of something!"

Mom suddenly got an idea. "I know what! Maybe you can get past the lookout dressed as cleaning women. There are clothes and buckets and mops downstairs," she whispered. "For gosh sakes, be careful."

"That's it!" cried Cherry. "Now, not a word, Mom." And with this word of caution, Cherry with Mildred close behind her, sped down to the basement.

There Cherry's eyes fell on some buckets, mops, and rags. She poked around in a closet and came out with some faded old cotton dresses and aprons. The girls donned the outfits and hurried to the inconspicuous back exit. Cherry whispered:

"I think we'd better talk in loud voices all the way over, and go sailing in. You'll see why in a minute. Come on! If only we can get in, we can worry then about what to do next. Just imitate everything I do and say. Understand?"

Out in the moonlit yard, in a direction opposite to the one Mildred had first taken, emerged two tattered blowsy figures, faces smudged. Their voices were shrill and their mop handles clattered and banged against their tin pails, as publicly as if it were broad daylight. They must have wakened a number of people near by.

They also had flashlights with which they seemed to be foolishly playing, whirling the long beams conspicuously around the yard and into the darkened windows of bedrooms.

As the two cleaning women drew close to the north side door of Lincoln Hall, chattering loudly, they were careful not to turn their flashlights on anyone who might be standing in the dark doorway. There was a rustle of movement in the doorway and the two girls quickened their footsteps. They made a sudden rush up the steps, found the door locked, used Mom's key, and hurled themselves inside.

"Whew!" Cherry whispered. She was trembling all over. She felt Mildred's cold hand groping for hers. They walked rapidly along the dark downstairs corridor. They reached a wall phone and Cherry looked at it longingly, but they passed on. They raced up the stairs, flashing their lights and peering closely. On the last flight, they made their steps loud and heavy and they talked loudly. They reached Dr. Joe's floor, the fourth floor, and stopped.

Cherry could feel her heart thumping slow and heavy and hard. She had a sick feeling in the pit of her stomach. The F.B.I. man was nowhere around. At the stairs she switched on, by a central floor control, all the lights of the corridor. The whole floor blazed with lights which could be seen from all over the yard, since the hall had front windows, here and there, between offices. Then Cherry walked down the corridor, almost dragging Mildred. Their mops and pails clanked, and their thumping footsteps echoed. But still there was no sign of the F.B.I. man. Cherry felt sure that something had happened to him.

The glass pane in the door of Dr. Joe's laboratory was dark. The thief probably was still there. The lookout might have signaled him. But the elevator was locked, there was only one central staircase, and they had not met anyone on their way up. No, he was still in there.

"Well, what d'you know!" the black-haired cleaning woman exclaimed shrilly. "Dr. Fortune's finally turned his light out! We won't go in there 'cause he might of fallen asleep in there again, like he does, the old curiosity! No ma'am, we'll stay out of Dr. Fortune's office! But I sure hope he don't come out here and track up our floor. We're going to git it good and clean if it takes us all night! Don't you forgit the janitor and Louie and Mr. Lane're coming up to see how good we do our jobs!"

Cherry then went to a sink in the corridor and turned the tap on full flood. It sounded like activity, and it gave her a moment to plan her next move. The man in there probably would not dare to come out into the hall now—unless he were a killer. He would not want to be waylaid by two women with heavy mops, who would later remember his face, and by the three men she said were coming here. He would not want to kill five people, even for the second page of that formula, if he could avoid it.

The only other way he could get out of that room now would be by rope. But a rope long enough to drop down four floors would make a huge suspicious bundle. He probably had not risked bringing anything so conspicuous with him. Lincoln Hall had no vines, no rough stones, no balconies, nothing the man could climb down on. Cherry and Mildred had him trapped in there.

But suppose, Cherry thought, he had a gun.

Cherry again said loudly, "That Dr. Fortune! He sure does work late hours. Well, we ain't goin' to go in and bother him—he's asleep for sure, in there. I hope he don't wake up and come out here and track up our floor the minute we've got it clean!"

Cherry abruptly turned off the water. In the sudden stillness, there was no sound from the room, no flash of light, no sound of pebbles nor a whistle from the lookout down in the yard, nothing. It looked as if the man was still in there. He surely must have heard them and their warning by now.

She and Mildred set up a great clatter with mops and pails and talk. Cherry carefully poured water beside Dr. Fortune's door and a stream eddied through into the laboratory. Every minute or so, she and Mildred suddenly would cease their racket and listen. Still there was not a sound. On a humid July night like this, they could have heard the faintest footstep, any creak of floor or window, the slightest rustle of movement, either in that room or down in the yard. She wished desperately that the police would come.

"Yes, ma'am!" Cherry declared loudly, banging her mop against her pail, "the janitor and those other two ought to be here any minute to inspect this grand clean hall! It's a shame we can't get in to clean the rooms, ain't it?"

They clattered and shrilled on, and Cherry wondered how much longer it was safe to keep this up. Why didn't someone come? The minutes seemed like hours. Mildred looked at Cherry beseechingly, her eyes terrified in her pale smudged face.

"Cheerio!" Cherry bawled with a grin. "How d'you like night life?" But her own hands were shaking, she was ice cold, and she was inwardly trembling with terror.

She *thought* she heard footsteps either downstairs or on the stairs. But she could not be *sure* she heard anything. Then there was a cry from the yard. Then Cherry heard men's loud angry voices, scuffling footsteps, a heavy door banging on the north side—they must have caught the lookout! At the same moment, five policemen burst into their corridor. They looked sharply at the two bogus cleaning women and Cherry silently pointed to Dr. Fortune's door. She and Mildred leaned against the wall and clung to each other as the police smashed and heaved and splintered the locked door. Just as the door fell, one of the policemen turned around.

"Get out of here fast!" he ordered them. "You might get shot up!"

Leaving their equipment where it lay, the two girls fled.

Cherry thought one wild thing as she ran. "If it's Lex in there, I don't want to see it!"

They ran to the open north side door. There was a knot of plainclothesmen and within the tight circle Cherry glimpsed a cowering man. A detective held out a powerful arm and blocked their path.

"Names?" he demanded. He turned a flashlight onto their faces.

"Cherry Ames, Mildred Burnham," Cherry gasped out.

"All right. Get going!"

It was a blessed relief to be out in the yard, outdoors, free again. They ran automatically for a few minutes, then they suddenly became weak and limp and could hardly walk. Somehow they dragged themselves to Crowley, and up to Cherry's floor. Sleepy nurses' heads stuck out of doors all along the hall.

"Ames, what happened? Look at you!"

"Are you all right, Cherry? Where were you in that dress?"

"You wakened the whole hospital! Why?"

"Mildred! Good grief, you two girls look like you've been through——"

"Please go back to your rooms, everybody!" Gwen took charge. "They're exhausted, let them alone! You'll hear about it in the morning." The nurses and students who had surged out into the hall all went quietly back into their rooms. Mildred was hanging on to Cherry, shaking violently. Cherry herself was in a trancelike state.

Gwen led them into her own room. "You're neither of you going back to your rooms tonight. Ann and I will stay with you for the rest of the night. You can sleep in here—if you can sleep."

Cherry and Mildred sank down onto chairs, too weak to care what Gwen was saying. Mildred burst into tears. Gwen led her to the bed, took off her shoes, and made her lie down. Cherry just sat with her head in her hands. She was too tired to figure out what was happening over there in Lincoln. Maybe it was all over by now. She hoped so. What a nasty business!

"You know, Mildred and I were lucky," she said absently.

"Lucky!" Gwen drew in her breath. "More than that! I was so scared for you when you left me that I—But I could see there was no stopping you!"

There was a kick at the door. Gwen opened it and Ann came in carrying a tray with a steaming pot of coffee and four cups. She took a quick, nurse's look at the two girls, and visibly relaxed. "Thank goodness for the kitchenette down the hall," she said. "Here, Cherry, drink this. I just told Mom that you—and everything—are all right. I wouldn't let her get up. Mildred—" Mildred accepted a cup. "Gwen, I think you and I have earned a cup of coffee, too."

"You certainly have," Cherry said gratefully. "Well, they got him. And that's all that matters."

Next morning Cherry was very tired. She felt as if she had lived ten years overnight. But she put on a clean crisp uniform and cap and went to take charge of her ward. She did not go to the nurses' dining room—she did not want to face all the questions. It was a bright beautiful summer morning, and here she was with her familiar patients, and the world seemed normal again—except for one thing. Would Lex appear on the ward today?

Gwen reported on duty. Mom, busy at work, had sent Cherry a pitifully relieved and grateful note. Cherry was glad that Mom's heartache was over.

"What did you hear?" Cherry asked Gwen anxiously.

They talked very low so that the patients would not overhear and be disturbed.

"I heard a lot," Gwen said. "In the first place, everyone asked for you. You're a heroine—you and your adoptee both. Mildred is quite a girl, isn't she?"

"She is indeed!" Cherry said warmly. "I'm just beginning to appreciate her. And Mom!—we could never have done it without Mom's help!" She added, "You and Ann deserve some credit too."

"We all won our share of fame," Gwen smiled, "and I must say it's a great nuisance. But the first thing you want to know is—it wasn't Lex! It wasn't anyone Lex ever could have been even remotely connected with! Lex is cleared, absolutely cleared."

Cherry ran her fingers through her curly black hair. "Lex is cleared," she repeated. "Lex is cleared." It took a minute or two for the words to sink in. She looked at Gwen gravely. "Practically this whole hospital owes him an apology. What a wretched time he's been through! No wonder he has been sullen and wouldn't talk. Poor Lex!"

"It's not 'poor' Lex any longer," Gwen reminded her cheerfully. "And now I'll tell you the rest. I'm not sure all the lurid details I heard are accurate, but here are the main facts. The police took the man at the door and the man in the lab. You already know that. The F.B.I. man had been knocked unconscious. The man in Dr. Fortune's office had a gun; there was quite a fight." Cherry felt the blood drain from her face. "There now," Gwen chided her, "do you see what a chance you took? He had the first page of the formula with him. They found a third man in a car, just outside the hospital grounds, with the motor running for a quick getaway. And after questioning and tracing some clues, about six o'clock this morning, the police broke into a hotel suite and found five other men. There was a whole ring of them. They all have police records—embezzlement, forgery, theft, assault. They wanted the drug for the tremendous amount of money it would bring."

"But—but did the police find the drug itself?" Cherry asked anxiously.

"That's a story all by itself. The men were too canny to leave it lying around a public hotel. They stored it in a safe deposit vault in a bank downtown. The police probably are taking it out right this minute."

"So the drug is safe," Cherry breathed, "and the formula too. Thank heaven for that!" She frowned, puzzling. "But who were these men—how did they ever stumble on Dr. Joe's drug in the first place?"

"Simple. It's so simple, it's startling. The man who was up in Dr. Joe's lab last night—gosh, I don't know where to begin." The redhead grinned. "That man was in State prison. He was in for murder, Cherry. Do you remember the jail break last winter? He was one of those who got away. He cut his hands and face pretty badly. So he came to our Out-Patient clinic for treatment, in spite of the fact that the police were searching for him. He told the police last night he figured he'd never be noticed in our big crowds of patients, and he was right. And while he was in and out of the clinic, our old friend gossip, plus all that publicity in the newspapers about penicillin, did the rest."

"I see," Cherry said, and her black eyes were very wide. She had read about murderers, and last night only a flimsy door and a mop had stood between her and a killer! She shuddered. But it was worth it in soldiers' lives—recovering that drug was worth anything! "The patient always comes first." "Save the patient at any cost to yourself." That was the nurse's creed!

Suddenly Cherry felt gay. "Won't Dr. Joe be happy?" she said to Gwen.

"I'll tell you who else is happy," Gwen said. She inclined her head toward the flagstone path. There was Lex hurrying toward the ward in the sunshine. He looked like a different young man. He was smiling for the first time in months, and that old lordly walk was his again.

"Cherry!" he called loudly. All the patients looked up. Lex hurried over to the head nurse's desk.

"Good morning, Dr. Upham," Cherry said demurely.

And then, to the patients' amazement, Dr. Upham put his arms around Head Nurse Ames and exuberantly whirled her around.

"You're cleared, Lex, you're cleared!" Cherry murmured over and over again.

"Thanks to you," he murmured back. Then he squared his big shoulders and pretended to roar, "Why aren't you all at work?" Gwen and everyone else scurried off in mock fear.

Then turning to Cherry, he said sternly, "As for you, Miss Ames, here are *your* orders. You are to go out on the lake with me tonight, young lady. Don't make that speech about how nurses are forbidden to have dates with staff doctors," he stopped her. "You've been telling me that all year. And don't argue with me!" Then relaxing his pose, he pleaded with her, "Surely a heroine like you would count as an exception! Please come, please?"

And rules or no rules, Cherry said, "Yes."

It was that magic part of evening when twilight softly steals its way across the earth. Out on the lake, Cherry sat back luxuriously as Lex spun their boat in great circles farther and farther out, until the ebbing sounds from shore were like dim music. He made a deft movement with an oar. The rowboat floated in one spot, water lapping gently at its sides.

"Nice here," Lex said unromantically, but Cherry knew what he meant. They sat quietly thinking for a while in the bobbing boat.

"Cherry," Lex finally spoke. "And now that the drug mystery is cleared up, we might as well make a clean sweep of everything. Here, read this!" He thrust Midge's trouble-making lollipop letter at her.

"I'm sorry—so sorry," she said as she read it for the first time. "You know I didn't talk to Midge about you."

"I should have known that," he agreed contritely. Lex smiled across at her. "So now all is forgiven?"

"Yes, Lex, all is *forgotten*," she smiled warmly back at him. She hesitated. "Except for one thing."

"What's that?"

"Lex, do you remember that afternoon in Dr. Joe's lab? That fateful day when Dr. Joe told us about the discovery?" He nodded his head. "Do you remember you said you couldn't take me to the Lincoln dance, that you had to work because you needed a lot of money?" He nodded again. "Why?" she asked softly.

Lex turned his face slightly. "So I could ask you a certain question."

"Oh!" Cherry exclaimed. They looked at each other gravely in the fading twilight. Then they both smiled. "Lex," Cherry said with difficulty, "please don't ask me that question. At least, don't ask it yet."

He said very low, "I'm in love with you, you know."

Cherry could only look at him with tender eyes. At last she found words. "That's wonderful, Lex. It makes me awfully happy—and sort of grateful." He was waiting for her to say more, to explain where he stood. She did not want to hurt him, but she had to tell him the truth. She chose her words with great feeling and care. "I don't know whether I'm in love with you or not, Lex. Honestly, I—I don't know." She stared out across the water. "But there's one thing I do know."

"Go on," Lex said steadily.

"It's this. I'm not ready to get married yet. I've barely finished my training and when I think about my future—my near future, that is—all I can see is me nursing somewhere. Gosh, I've trained and trained! I want to have a try at it!"

"To tell you the truth," Lex admitted, and there was the hint of a chuckle in his voice, "I feel somewhat the same way. I haven't been a full-fledged doctor very long, and I'm in a hurry to get plenty of practice under my belt."

Cherry gave him a grateful smile. "Thanks for saying that. I don't feel quite so badly now. You see how it is—for instance, though an Army nurse can marry, she might not be stationed near her husband, so that——"

"I didn't know you were planning to be an Army nurse," he interrupted.

That pulled Cherry up short. "I didn't know it myself—I *don't* know it, I mean, I haven't decided." But from what she had just said, she must have been thinking of Army nursing more seriously than she realized. "Are you going into the service, Lex? Into the Medical Corps?"

"I think so."

They were silent for a while. Night began to fall and shadows deepened. "We'd better get back to shore," Lex said.

"Wait. There's one more thing I want to say."

He leaned forward on the oars to listen. Cherry said very gently and deliberately:

"Lex, you didn't propose to me. So I couldn't say either yes or no, could I? Nothing has been said, really. We're just where we always were. Agreed?"

"Agreed!" He added, "You're a wise girl, Cherry."

The boat started to float forward. The oars dipped and rose, dipped and rose, leaving a murmurous white trail of foam. They disappeared softly into the spacious night.

CHAPTER XIV

Day of Glory

SOMETHING EXTRAORDINARY HAD COME OVER THE SENIORS. Here it was August with examinations and, hopefully, graduation nearly upon them. They were studying like mad, they worked like Trojans on their wards, they had no idea where they would be next month. "But we're so hilarious," Cherry remarked to Ann and Gwen, "I'd say we were drunk—drunk on the prospect of wearing white almost any day now!"

And after they had taken their final examinations, there was no holding them, even though State examinations would come soon after graduation. They were the glorious seniors standing on the brink of their careers and the wide world! The hospital was theirs!

One of the traditions at Spencer had to be carried out the night before the triumphant seniors first appeared with the black bands of the graduate nurse. And that night it had to rain. Sheets of warm rain beat down fiercely, almost like a tropical storm. The seniors pressed their faces against the dining room windows after supper, and hesitated.

"We're going anyway," Cherry announced. "Here's where black stockings and Ames part company!"

Her classmates debated between the hated black stockings and the weather. In the end they buttoned themselves into their raincoats. The wind and the rain lashed the trees in the yard, and the lake was dark and wild. The crowd of girls pushed their way to the water's edge.

"First!" Cherry cried, and sat down in the dripping grass. She untied her oxfords, pulled off her stockings, then ran barefoot to the water. "Good-by forever!" she cried and hurled her stockings into the lake.

Beside her, half crouched in the rain, Gwen brandished her black stockings around her head like a lasso. "Here you go!" she yelled, and in went Gwen's stockings.

Cherry stood around shivering and laughing as the whole big class filled the lake with black cotton stockings. They returned to Spencer barelegged but happy.

The next day the sun shone down brightly on the happy seniors. They made their first appearance with the broad black velvet band on the cuff of their caps—badge of the graduate nurse. Cherry felt as if she were clothed in glory, for this was the public symbol of her success. All day long Cherry was overwhelmed with congratulations from everybody. The whole hospital seemed to be rejoicing with the seniors. As if all that happiness were not enough, Cherry found in her room at Crowley a great bouquet of roses from Lex and Dr. Joe together, and a telegram from her parents and Midge. "Hurray for Nurse Ames," it read, "we are coming graduation day."

In the midst of all this excitement, three newspaper reporters arrived to interview Cherry Ames, R.N.— well, R.N. any moment now. The interview took place in Dr. Joe's now-famous laboratory. Cherry answered a landslide of questions, with Lex and Dr. Joe and Mom and Mildred proudly exclaiming how wonderful she was. Cherry was annoyed at this personal angle. What really mattered was that the drug was safe! It all came out in the newspapers, alongside a picture of Cherry which made her face look as though it had been through a mangle. "Quick-Witted Young Nurse Saves Priceless Military Drug," said the headlines, and "Faces Murderer So Soldiers May Live." Cherry went through a lot of good-natured teasing to live that one down.

Another Spencer tradition was that the graduating seniors "bequeathed" their personal belongings to the younger students who were staying on at the hospital.

Cherry had not realized how popular she was until at least twenty younger girls started begging her to "leave" them *her* things. Cherry shared the cushions which dressed up her daybed between the two first-year students on her ward. To Lucy, the maid on Children's Ward, Cherry gave her alarm clock. For the many others, she found little knick-knacks around her room—book ends, a gay pincushion, a vase. To Mom, she gave her silk comforter and her little radio. But it was to Mildred that Cherry gave her most personal things—her soft goose feather bed pillow from home, the little lamp on her bedside table, her books. There were tears in Mildred's eyes when Cherry piled all these things into her arms.

"I don't want you to go away, Cherry," she said.

"I'll write," Cherry promised. "I'll want to know how you're getting along and you'll have to write me all the Spencer news."

"Where will you be?"

"I don't know," Cherry had to reply. In a matter of hours, she would be out of here and she still did not know where she was going. Neither did most of her classmates. Vivian Warren had had an offer from a small city hospital, but Vivian wanted a better-paying position to make up for her years of hardship and unremitting work. Bertha had been invited to be visiting nurse in her own rural community. Cherry herself could easily have secured a post through Dr. Joe or Miss Reamer or on her own application. But like all the rest of her class-mates, she was putting off the decision. She was still thinking earnestly about Army nursing.

Two nights before graduation day the seniors had to attend the final lecture. It was late when they came out and headed back toward Crowley. Suddenly a huge crowd of student nurses surged around them from all sides. They had been lying in wait! Laughing, they fell upon the outnumbered seniors and proceeded to tear off the seniors' blue and white student dresses, their student aprons and bibs! They left them in their caps and very little else. Cherry fled into Crowley just in time to escape with her slip.

The next day Cherry and her class appeared proudly in all-white. She thought she would burst with pride. She had earned it, and it was hers to wear for the rest of her life! In another way, Cherry felt very sober. Here she was at the ending. No, this was not an ending, for she stood again at the beginning of something new—whatever it might be.

Early that afternoon the seniors left in giggling groups for the photographer's. They came back to attend Miss Reamer's tea for the seniors. When they walked in, they exclaimed—the familiar lounge looked so festive, with great bowls of colorful flowers everywhere and a sumptuous tea table. A number of the doctors and supervisors and head nurses and surgeons with whom they had worked had come to do them honor. Even some of the Administrators of Spencer Hospital were present, and Cherry actually regretted Dr. Wylie's absence. The visiting and the tea that followed were very pleasant. After an hour, the others left and only the guests of honor, the seniors, and Miss Reamer remained.

The Superintendent of Nurses sat down beside the flower-banked fireplace and looked from one radiant young face to another. "When you all first came to Spencer," she said with a smile, "I told you you had the makings of an exceptional class. I was not mistaken. I expect big things of this class. And now I must tell you something about the careers which are open to you, although I have already talked to each of you individually. If you ever want to consult me again, come back to Spencer, no matter how many years after graduation." Cherry smiled at her gratefully and Miss Reamer smiled back.

Cherry was astonished at the length of Miss Reamer's list. Nurses were needed now, and would be needed in even greater numbers after the war, Miss Reamer said—as general duty nurses in great city hospitals—as private duty nurses, pleasant work which could take them all over the world—as those invaluable community guardians, public health nurses, Red Cross nurses—as rural nurses driving a clinic on wheels, bringing health care to farmers and people in isolated communities—as children's nurses—the list went on and on.

"There is something for every taste, you see," Miss Reamer smiled. "City or small town or country, at home or abroad, big crowds or a handful of people, young or old."

Miss Reamer stopped for breath and so did the seniors. Gwen sprang up and presented her with an enormous pitcher of iced tea. Everybody laughed.

"A glass would be nice," Miss Reamer hinted to Gwen. Gwen produced one. The class waited, then the Superintendent of Nurses went on again:

"Then there are, as I hardly need tell you, Army and Navy nurses. Just now, that is the most needed and gallant work of all. That most likely would take you to far parts of the world, and you'd certainly be helping in making history. And it won't be a temporary wartime job. After the war, there will be plenty of veterans' nursing to be done. There also will be relief and rehabilitation programs in the war-torn countries, and nurses will be needed to help those starved people back to health again." She smiled at them. "I think I've finally finished, believe it or not!"

After some questions, and some informal talking-it-over, the seniors drifted down to the lake. Their adoptees, just turned juniors, were fêting them with a picnic.

Down at the water's edge it was still bright afternoon at six-thirty. The adoptees had set up a picnic table, spread with huge bowls of potato salad and baked beans and tomatoes and dill pickles. The frankfurters already sizzling over an open bonfire smelled tantalizing. The seniors were not allowed to help, so some of them, at Cherry's light-hearted suggestion, went wading. The hot dogs, on toasted buns, tasted every bit as good as they smelled. And with the steaming coffee, their adoptees proudly brought forth a vast tiered cake. It was decorated with the senior's class flower, gardenias, made of sparkling white spun icing.

"Are you enjoying it?" Mildred asked Cherry eagerly.

"It's divine!" Cherry replied. "It's something I'll look back on and wish could happen again!"

After supper, they sat on the grass or leaned against tree trunks and watched the sun drop lower and lower toward the rim of the lake. Someone started to sing. Then everyone was singing familiar songs—rollicking ones, dreamy ones. They sang until the first star flickered in the pale sky, and shadows crossed their faces. A huge orange harvest moon rose slowly out of the treetops. Suddenly, as though at a given signal, the group began to sing the school song—slow, grave, and yet ringing:

All o'er the earth
Angels in white,

In sickness, age, and birth,
Bring light.

Healing we bring,
Hope and help we bring,
We of Spencer too shall bring,
These brave and shining deeds we sing–
Our sister, our Nurse!

It was a pledge and an ideal. The last note of the sweet clear girls' voices died away among the trees. They started to gather up their picnic things. Cherry realized sadly that her student days were over.

CHAPTER XV

Cherry Decides

GRADUATION DAY STARTED AT SIX O'CLOCK IN THE morning for Cherry, when the phone shrilled in Crowley corridor.

"Good morning, dear. Congratulations!" said a familiar cheerful voice.

"Mother!" Cherry said. She was suddenly very happy. "Mother, where are you?"

"Hi, Cherry!" came Midge's voice. "Aren't you excited? Isn't it wonderful! I'm dying to see you in your white get-up!"

"Will someone kindly tell me where you all are?" Cherry demanded, laughing.

Her father's voice came over the receiver. "How is the graduate? We're here at the railroad station and we're going to have some breakfast. What time do you want us up there?"

"Graduation is at noon, Dad, but please come as soon as you can!"

Shortly after she had hung up, the phone rang again. Cherry raced down the corridor for the second time.

It was Charlie. "Sorry, I can't tell you where I am. But it's a long way from where you are. . . . I'm fine. . . . Look here, I didn't call up long distance to talk about me. . . . Well, I'm not permitted to tell anything over the phone, anyway. . . . Yes, I *am* fine, and congratulations! I'm pretty proud of my twin sister. . . . Good for you! . . . That's right, we're both doing the things we always had our hearts set on. . . . I'll bet. . . . I sure would like to see you. . . . Not a chance. . . . We might meet up by accident on the other side of the world. . . . Yes, I got your letter. Let me know what you decide, will you? . . . Say, my three minutes are up! Write me. . . . Congratulations again and I mean it! . . . So long— Nurse!"

Cherry hung up with a hand that trembled a little. It would be strange, having a graduation without Charlie around. They had always had their graduations together. What a darling he was to phone!

She missed him acutely when her parents arrived and they were all together except for Charlie. But she remembered *he* was all alone and probably twice as lonesome. And her mother looked so charming, her father was so obviously proud of her, and Midge was so thrilled, that Cherry was as happy as seniors are meant to be on graduation day.

Presently Cherry, in her dazzling white uniform and cap, had quite a group gathered around her in the lounge. Her parents, Midge, Dr. Joe, Lex, Mildred, and even Mom was there. She beamed when Cherry said, "Mom helped us catch the penicillin thief!" By the time Cherry had introduced some of her classmates, and had been introduced to their families, and taken her mother to see her room at Crowley, and then returned to the lounge, it was time for the seniors to assemble. Cherry's guests went into the auditorium and Cherry, with Ann and Gwen, hurried to the smaller room beside the auditorium.

The seniors took their places in a long line four abreast. These were the last few minutes they all would be together as a class. In an hour from now, Cherry would no longer be a student. Her class would be breaking up, and the girls she had worked and played and lived with for three years would scatter to the four corners of the globe. Cherry wondered if she would ever see any of them again. The girls were trying to joke, but their eyes were sad and their voices unsteady.

"Have you decided what you're going to do yet, Cherry?" Ann asked her very low.

Cherry shook her head. "No, not yet," she whispered back.

Ann straightened her shoulders and stared ahead. Cherry knew what Ann's plans were, and Mai Lee's, and a number of others'. It would be only a few moments more now . . .

There was a rustle of starched white uniforms. Cherry looked around and saw the Superintendent of Nurses coming past the rows of graduates, accompanied by two women. One was an Army Nurse, the other a Red Cross Nurse.

When they reached the front of the room, Miss Reamer raised her hand and called the class to attention.

"Graduates," she addressed them. "I take pleasure in introducing to you Miss Culver from the Red Cross. She has a message for you."

Miss Culver smiled and stepped forward. She spoke briefly but with deep feeling. "I am here to help appeal to you to answer our country's urgent need for war nurses. But we have with us someone who can tell you even better than I just how crying that need is. May I present to you Lieutenant Sanders, one of the Army Nurses who escaped from Corregidor."

The Army Nurse, trim and neat in her uniform, greeted the graduates, who were watching her intently with eager, expectant faces. "I hardly know how or where to begin . . . there's so much to tell!" In her face was reflected all the horror and suffering she had seen—landing barges full of sick and wounded; boys lying fever-ridden and helpless in jungle hospitals; doctors working tirelessly day and night, often without a nurse to help. A note of urgency crept into her voice as she pleaded with them to answer their country's call. "You are needed, desperately needed! If we are to save our men out there fighting for us—if we are even to win this war—you nurses must help. Are you ready to serve?"

Cherry and her classmates had heard other appeals. But this appeal was different. It was being put directly up to each one of them. For the first time, Cherry felt personally responsible for the lives of Charlie and all the other American boys.

Beside her there was a crackle of a sleeve. Ann had raised her hand. She could hear Ann's quickened breathing. Mai Lee's hand was raised next. The room was filled with tension and a breathless silence. Cherry watched with her heart pounding. Then Bertha Larsen's hand went up; Marie Swift's; Gwen's; Vivian's. Then five more hands shot up, one after another. No one had said a word, and still no one spoke.

"What shall I do?" Cherry thought frantically. "How can I let them go and not go too? Those boys I saved Dr. Joe's drug for—" Out of the hush, hands were slowly raised, until it seemed a white forest blurred Cherry's vision. "Those soldiers who needed the drug—" suddenly she realized that she had faced a murderer because she felt responsible for those boys—way down deep, she had thought of them as her patients! That was her answer!

Cherry raised her hand.

The room was profoundly silent. Miss Reamer's face was working with emotion. The two nurses preserved their quiet expressions but their eyes were shining. It was unanimous. The whole graduating class had volunteered.

The silence seemed to be swelling and growing, as if the room would burst, and out of it they suddenly were singing, "We too shall bring . . . " as they had never sung it before! Miss Reamer wiped her eyes.

Shaken, the class marched into the auditorium, to the grave music of the organ. They took their seats on the platform. Ranks and ranks of them in white, they looked out at the familiar loving faces in the audience. Cherry found her father and mother. Lex sat next to them, beaming up at Cherry.

The Red Cross Nurse was talking to the audience, " . . . all of these young women have volunteered! Unanimously! All of them are making the greatest offering any woman can." A roar of applause rolled forward like thunder.

The graduation exercises were dignified and simple. The names of the graduates were read, and in a sort of dream Cherry walked across the platform and Miss Reamer presented her with her certificate.

"Good luck, Cherry!" she said.

Cherry sat down again, trembling. She was a nurse now! She was really a nurse!

Then all of a sudden it was all over and Cherry was down off the stage with her parents and friends. They were embracing her and congratulating her, both on her graduation and on her great decision, although Cherry's mother had tears in her eyes as she smiled.

Here they were, all the dear familiar faces—her sweet mother, her good, kind father, Midge and Mildred both looking toward her with the shining wistful admiration of younger girls, here were Mom and her beloved Dr. Joe, and Lex with his serious gaze, redheaded Gwen, and Ann, not calm for once, her classmates and her teachers.

But Cherry saw beyond them. She was looking into the exciting, unknown future which stretched ahead of her. She, Cherry Ames, was going to be an Army Nurse!